Corinne
to the Rescue

By Wendy Wan-Long Shang
Illustrated by Peijin Yang

★ American Girl®

Published by American Girl Publishing

22 23 24 25 26 27 28 QP 10 9 8 7 6 5 4 3 2 1

This book is a work of fiction. Any similarity to real persons, living or dead, is coincidental and not intended by American Girl. References to real events, people, or places are used fictitiously. Other names, characters, places, and incidents are the products of imagination.

Illustrations by Peijin Yang
Cover image by Peijin Yang · Book design by Gretchen Becker

The following individuals and organizations have generously granted permission to reproduce their photographs: pp. 129–132—Courtesy of Jennifer Jerabek; pp. 134–135—David Roth. All rights reserved.

Cataloging-in-Publication Data available from the Library of Congress

Not all services are available in all countries.

Dedicated to

LJF, who keeps
me laughing
—W.S.

Arne and Mom

Cassidy, Gwynn, Flurry, Corinne

Flurry

Corinne, Gwynn, Dad

With gratitude to:

Greta Gessele, professional figure skating instructor in Aspen. Greta started skating at age six and grew up competing and performing with the Aspen Skating Club.

Dr. Jennifer Ho, professor of ethnic studies at the University of Colorado Boulder and president of the Association for Asian American Studies (2020–2022).

Angela Liu, digital marketing manager at American Girl and member of American Girl's diversity task force.

Lori Spence, director, Aspen Highlands Ski Patrol and avalanche dog trainer. Lori currently works with a black Labrador retriever named Meka.

Dr. William Wei, professor of modern Chinese history at the University of Colorado Boulder, and 2019–2020 Colorado State Historian.

Contents

The Last Snow

Chapter 1

*S*pring in Aspen makes me feel mixed up. On the one
hand, I like the longer sunny days, the flowers coming
up, and the chance to switch out of long pants and sweat-
ers. On the other hand, melting patches of snow are kind
of ugly and dirty-looking and not much good for skiing.
On the other-other hand, spring melt means that summer
vacation is coming.

See what I mean about feeling mixed up?

Today, Dad came to pick up me and my sister, Gwynn,
for our weekend visit. My parents are divorced, and
Gwynn and I live with our mother and stepdad, Arne.
Because my dad is a ski instructor and is really busy in the
winter, springtime means that he has more time for Gwynn
and me. That's another good thing about spring.

"Let's hit Buttermilk one more time!" said Dad. "I think
this is the last good day for skiing." Buttermilk is the name
of the ski resort where my dad works.

I felt a little pang in my heart. I love skiing, the way

Corinne to the Rescue

I glide down the mountain and feel fast and sleek while looking at the snow and sky and trees. Gwynn saw my face and put her hand in mine. We call it sister brain—knowing what the other person is thinking without saying anything.

"Don't be sad," said Gwynn. "When we can't ski, we can do other things. We can go swimming and hiking and biking and canoeing and camping and . . ." Lately, Gwynn's new thing has been making lists out loud.

"Yes!" I said, trying to share her enthusiasm. "And sleeping in! And Five New Things!"

Five New Things is our summer tradition. We have to learn or try five new things together. Last year, we:

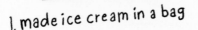

1. made ice cream in a bag

2. sledded on sand at Great Sand Dunes National Park

3. sewed our own tote bags

4. ate dinner inside an old airplane that's been turned into a restaurant

5. tried Korean barbecue

The Last Snow

But that was all before Mom and Arne got married. Normally Mom, Gwynn, and I picked the Five New Things. Now I wondered if Arne would get to pick one, too.

That was also before we got my dog, Flurry. She should have a chance to try Five New Things, too! And I'd have plenty of time to spend with her when school was out. I was training Flurry to be an avalanche dog, a dog that finds people lost in the snow. She had already rescued one person over the winter—*me*! I'll never forget the feeling I got when she found me—like relief and happiness rolled into one. Flurry and I had bonded as soon as I met her at the shelter, but after the rescue, we really were a team. I wanted our team to get even better.

Which brought me back to my mixed-up feelings. How could I practice rescue skills with Flurry without snow?

"Can we bring Flurry to Buttermilk?" I asked Dad.

"If we bring Flurry, we can't go downhill skiing," said Dad. "It's not safe." Dad wasn't saying no, not exactly.

I felt so torn. I wanted to go skiing, but I also wanted to practice with Flurry one more time in the snow. Thinking of everything as *the last time* gave me a twisty feeling in my stomach.

"Wait," said Dad. "What if we go to the freestyle park near the ski school instead? There's an easy rail there to practice on. We can take turns holding Flurry." Freestyle skiing is an acrobatic form of skiing and includes skiing on half-pipes, rails, and other equipment.

I gave Dad a hug. He has the best ideas! "Yes! That's perfect." Dad had been teaching us the basics of freestyle skiing, like switch skiing, which means skiing backward, and buttering, which means popping off the slope and rotating in the air. Now we could try out our skills.

"I can name the different types of jibs," announced Gwynn. A jib is something you can ski on. "Flat box, flat rail, bonk, rainbow, wall ride . . ."

"Are you going to ski them all?" asked Dad, which thankfully stopped Gwynn from making another list.

"I'm gonna try!" said Gwynn.

"Should we count this toward our Five New Things?" I asked. Under the rules of Five New Things, it had to be new for at least two people.

"We usually don't count until after school lets out," said Gwynn.

"Yes, but they're our rules," I said.

Gwynn nodded vigorously. "Then yes!"

🌲🌲🌲

When we got to the park, Gwynn skied right up to the rail, jumped up, and immediately banged into the rail and fell backward.

The Last Snow

"Are you okay, Gwynn?" said Dad.

Gwynn nodded, embarrassed. "It looks so easy when other people do it," she said.

"It wasn't a bad first try," said Dad. He turned to me. "Do you want to give it a go? See what you can do on your own?"

"Sure!" I handed Flurry's leash to Dad and skied to the same rail. I gathered up a bit of speed, eyed the rail, bent my knees, and glided down the rail.

"Great job!" said Dad. He was beaming.

Gwynn, however, was not happy. "That's not fair!" she grumbled. "How come you did it perfectly, and I fell on my face?"

"I'm older than you," I reminded her. "I've skied more than you have."

"Yeah, but . . . but . . ." Gwynn stammered.

"You're better at skating than I am," I told her. "You've been working so hard at it and practicing so many hours. I wouldn't be able to do half the things you do on the ice."

"I guess," said Gwynn. She put her hands on her hips and glared at the rail, as if the rail had tricked her.

"It looked like you might have been going a little too slow," Dad said. "You need a certain amount of speed to make it onto the rail."

"That seems scarier," said Gwynn. "Going faster."

"You know how in skating you need some speed to

make a jump? It's the same thing," I explained

Gwynn put her chin down and tried again. This time she was going so fast that she flew completely over the rail instead of landing on it and gliding down.

"You'll get it," I told her. "Now you know what's too fast and too slow." Gwynn took off her goggles, pushed her hair out of her face, and sighed.

I didn't want Gwynn to feel bad about the rail. "Why don't you and Dad work on this, and I'll take Flurry over there to work on rescues?" I had spotted a nice, thick pile of snow, shielded from the sun by some trees.

"Are you sure?" asked Dad.

"I'm sure," I said. "I want to work with Flurry before all the snow melts, remember?"

"All right," said Dad. "Just stay in sight, okay?" I promised to stay close.

I had brought along an old stinky T-shirt of Arne's, which I showed to Flurry. Then I had Flurry sit and stay, facing away from the area where I wanted her to work. I buried Arne's T-shirt in the snow, smoothing the snow with my hand so she wouldn't have any clues. I marched all over the area and called Dad and Gwynn over, too. They walked around for a bit and then went back to the rail. This was a test for Flurry, to see if she could find the shirt among all the other smells.

The Last Snow

"Go on, Flurry. Search!" Flurry stood up and wagged her tail. "You've got this! Find Arne's shirt!"

Flurry's nose twitched and made little huffing noises. I'd read that dogs can smell in layers—their smells don't get mixed up like they do for people. I wondered what the area smelled like to her. Could she smell laundry detergent on the shirt? Arne's deodorant? She lowered her head and investigated the area. Slowly, she moved away from where the shirt was buried, and my heart sank. Maybe I'd made this too hard.

But then she sniffed the spot where I had laid the shirt while I dug the hole. She worked her way back to the right place. Suddenly, Flurry rose on her hind legs and plunged her front feet into the snow. She began digging. Her head disappeared into the snow, her tail wagging furiously, and she emerged with the T-shirt in her mouth.

"Good girl!" I ran over and praised her. "You did it!

You did it!" We played tug-of-war with the shirt as a reward. "Flurry's a good girl! Yes she is! Good search!" I probably sounded ridiculous, but I didn't care. The important part was encouraging Flurry.

"Well, look who's here!" I turned

and saw two adults—a woman and a man. I knew the man—it was Zach! Zach is my dad's friend who works with search and rescue dogs. He had helped me train Flurry.

"Hi, Zach!" I snapped Flurry's leash back on and went over to them. "Look, Flurry, it's Zach!"

"Good work out there," said Zach. "I see you're keeping up with the training we talked about." He turned to the woman standing next to him. "Kim, this is Corinne. She's the girl I was telling you about, the one whose dog found her on Ajax." Ajax is the nickname for Aspen Mountain, one of the mountains surrounding Aspen.

"Nice to meet you, Corinne," said Kim. "Looks like you're doing great work."

"Thanks! I want to keep up her training, but I'm not sure how once the snow melts."

"Well?" Zach turned to Kim to see what she would say. "Kim is my dog-training mentor," he explained.

"Mentor?" The only word I knew that sounded like mentor was *Dementor*, from Harry Potter, and that was not a good thing. Kim looked nice, though. She had pretty silver hair and eyes that crinkled when she smiled.

"A mentor is someone who guides you and helps you make good decisions," said Zach. "They give you the benefit of their knowledge and experience. Kim gave me advice on what to do when my dog got hurt and needed rehab."

The Last Snow

Having a mentor sounded pretty cool.

Dad spotted Zach and came over with Gwynn to say hello. Kim squatted and scratched Flurry around her ears. "There are lots of things you can do to keep up her training without snow."

"Like what?" I asked.

"First, make sure she gets well socialized and can get along with other dogs. We don't want dogs to get into fights," said Kim. "Walk around town with her, and make sure she knows how to heel and doesn't jump on people."

"Okay," I said. "What else?"

"Make sure you keep playing hide-and-seek with her," said Kim. "And take her out on hikes and runs. She needs to stay in shape. Searching is hard work."

"What else?" I asked.

"What else?" Kim looked surprised.

Dad chuckled. "Corinne is pretty determined about her dog training. Flurry rescued her when she was lost."

Kim smiled, like she was impressed with how serious I was about training Flurry. "Well, for a summer rescue, she'll need to be able to hop into an all-terrain vehicle to reach remote areas of the forest," Kim said. "Can she load onto a ski lift?"

"No, not yet," I said. We hadn't been able to practice the "load up" command because only ski patrol dogs are allowed on the lifts during the ski season. "Though I tell her to load up when I call her onto the couch or my bed." I was proud of knowing some of the commands that search and rescue used.

"That's a start! Can she climb on your back?" Kim asked. "Sometimes we carry our dogs that way to help save their strength and energy."

"I haven't tried that one yet," I told her.

"Hmm. Has she ever ridden in a sled?" Kim asked. "We don't use sleds in the summer, of course, but she might need to ride in something similar, like a boat."

"Like a canoe?" I asked, excitedly. "I love canoeing! I bet I could train Flurry how to ride in one."

"That works," said Kim. "So, the deal is that when Flurry here can do those things, you tell me, and I'll take you out for practice with us, okay? And who knows? Maybe after that, an actual rescue search."

"Are you serious?" I asked. I couldn't believe that Kim was making this offer. "That would be amazing!"

"We'll have to ask Mom, too," said Dad. "But I think it'd be okay."

"I am serious," said Kim. "But it's a lot for you and your dog to learn. And there are a lot of steps to get from here to there. How about we plan to chat in a few weeks and see how your training is coming along?"

The Last Snow

"Is this something that, um, my parents pay you for?" I asked, suddenly shy. I hadn't thought of that until now.

"No," said Kim. "Someone helped me out, and now I'm helping you. One day, you'll help someone else. That's all I ask for. Pay it forward."

Sister Squeeze

Chapter 2

I couldn't wait to get started on training Flurry with Kim's new goals, and I knew the perfect place to begin. Last year, Arne's interior decorator had designed a bedroom for Gwynn and me. The room was beautiful. It looked like a ski chalet, with cozy bunk beds and a fireplace you could turn on with a switch. The walls had mountains painted on them, and an old ski chairlift hung from the ceiling.

I had practiced the command "load up" with Flurry, but never on the chairlift. The one in our room was from a long time ago, so it was small with a wooden seat instead of sleek and metal all over, but it would be good for practice.

As soon as Dad dropped off Gwynn and me at Mom and Arne's house, I ran upstairs with Flurry to my room. We could try loading up right away! Except when I opened the door, I discovered that Gwynn had covered the chairlift in stuffed animals before we'd left. They were strapped into the seat and attached to the sides with belts and scarves.

Sister Squeeze

Gwynn came into the room. "Gwynn!" I said. "What is this?"

"The animals are going for a ride. To the top of the moon," said Gwynn, as if it were obvious.

"And they're all harnessed in?" I asked.

"For safety, while we were gone," said Gwynn. "I didn't want anything to happen to Philomena or Sam or Fernanda or Jack or Michaelina or Bob or Stephanie the Second or Joe . . ." For some reason, Gwynn gave all her girl stuffed animals really long names and all her boy stuffed animals really short names. Also, she had a lot of them.

"Please don't list all your animals," I said. I gestured toward the lift. "I wanted to practice loading on the chair-lift with Flurry."

"So what do you want me to do?" asked Gwynn.

"I was kind of hoping you could clear it off," I said. "So I could use it."

Gwynn walked over to the chair and unbuckled a purple kangaroo. "Come, Philomena," she said gloomily. "The trip to the moon is over." She walked Philomena over to her bed and set her down. Then she untied a scarf and released a blue bunny. "Come, Bob," she said. "The trip to the moon is over."

This was going to take a while.

Arne appeared in the doorway. "Hello, girls," he said.

"Did you have fun at your dad's?"

"Yes," said Gwynn. "But now Cori is making my animals end their trip to the moon." She sighed dramatically as she untied another stuffed animal.

"It's for a training project. With Flurry," I said. "Where's Mom?" I couldn't wait to tell her about meeting Kim.

"She's interviewing people for the restaurant."

Mom runs a Chinese street food restaurant called Kuai Le. It just opened a few months ago, but it's already very popular, which was why Mom was hiring help. I asked if I could walk over to the shop, and Arne said it was okay.

🌲🌲🌲

At the restaurant, I tied Flurry to a tree outside and poked my head in. I was lucky—Mom was alone.

"Hi, Mom!"

"Corinne!" said Mom from one of the tables. "I'm just taking a little break between interviews. Come in! Look what someone just dropped off!" She held out her hand, and something long and golden dangled down.

I took a closer look and gasped. "Gwynn's necklace!" Last winter, Gwynn and I had made a sister shrine on the mountain. Aspen is full of hidden shrines, which are trees decorated to celebrate people like Elvis Presley or comic strip characters like Calvin and Hobbes. Gwynn and I made a shrine just for us. Gwynn had insisted on adding the necklace from Arne, because the shrine needed to be more special. The time Flurry rescued me, I'd gotten lost on the mountain looking for our shrine and the necklace.

"How did they know to bring it here?" I asked.

"There aren't too many Gwynns in this town," said Mom. Gwynn's name was engraved on a charm on her necklace. I had one with my name engraved on it, too. "But the kicker is that a tag from Kuai Le was still tangled up in the necklace, so they brought it here. I'm amazed that the tag didn't blow away!"

"Gwynn will be so happy!" I said. This seemed like a good sign. "I have some cool news, too." I told her about meeting Kim, and her offer to be my mentor.

Mom nodded, impressed. "Of course I'm okay with that, as long as you think you and Flurry are ready to learn those skills," said Mom.

"I was thinking we could take Flurry with us when we go camping, so she can practice riding in a canoe! That would count as one of the Five New Things because we've never gone camping and canoeing with a dog, and Flurry hasn't done those things before!" Camping and canoeing were our summer traditions, but adding a twist, like sleeping in a hammock, counted as a new thing.

Mom got a funny look on her face. "Well, we haven't

really talked about going camping this year," she said.

"But we go every summer!" I said. I wondered why Mom was making a weird expression. "It doesn't have to count as a new thing, since we've done it before," I said. Maybe Mom had other ideas for our Five New Things.

"Oh, I'm not worried about that part," said Mom. She smiled. "I think we'll find lots of new things to try this summer!"

Flurry barked from outside.

"You and Flurry should get to work," said Mom. "And I have my next interview in a few minutes. See you at dinner, okay?"

🌲🌲🌲

When Flurry and I got back home, Gwynn had cleared off the chairlift and was playing a video game. I sat down on the wooden seat and called to Flurry. "Load up, Flurry!" I said, patting the spot next to me. The chair wiggled a little. It hung from the ceiling and was pretty solid, but you could still feel it move.

Flurry put one paw on the seat and started panting. I could see why she was nervous. It wouldn't be easy for her to turn around on the narrow seat once she climbed up, and the seat was slippery. Still, I had to try. "Come on, girl," I said. I took one of her toys, a puffy lamb, and held it up in the air so she'd have to use the chairlift to get to it. Flurry put a second paw on the seat and poked at me with her nose. Then she sat down on the floor and looked up at me uneasily.

"Like this, Flurry!" Gwynn nudged Flurry to one side and hopped into the seat next to me. She bent her hands forward and pretended to be a dog. "Woof woof!" She pretended to grab for the lamb.

Normally Gwynn made me laugh, but this time I didn't appreciate it. "Please don't interrupt, Gwynnie." I leaned forward and stroked Flurry's head. "We're in the middle of a training session."

"She doesn't want to sit here," said Gwynn. "I can tell."

"She doesn't want to *yet*," I said. "We'll

get there." I turned my attention back to Flurry.

Gwynn slid onto the floor so she was lying next to Flurry. "Can we play a game?" she asked.

"Maybe after my session with Flurry," I said. "But you have to let us work. Flurry needs to learn this so we can go on a search and rescue practice with Kim."

"It's my room, too," said Gwynn.

Our room at Arne's had always been big enough for the both of us. We even had a walk-in closet. But now the walls seemed to be closing in.

"Please, Gwynn?" I asked. "Just, like, five or ten minutes."

Gwynn stood up, walked into the hallway, and sprawled on the floor in the doorway. "I'm leaving you alone now."

"You're in the doorway," I said.

"I'm not in the room," said Gwynn.

I guessed that was the best I was going to get. I got up and stood next to the chairlift so there would be more room on the seat for Flurry. "Load up, Flurry!" I said. Flurry put her front paws on the seat and then tried to add her back paws, but she was shaking, which made the chair shake. She lowered herself back to the floor. I could see that she was torn between staying safe and making me happy. I put my leg against the chair to hold it still. Flurry put her two front paws on the seat again and tried to give me a kiss. It was like she was saying, *Don't be mad! I'm just not ready!*

"I'm not mad at you girl," I said, stroking her ears. "Don't worry."

"Yeah," called Gwynn. "Cori's mad at *me*!"

"I'm not," I said to Gwynn. But in my head I added, *Not that much!*

Surprises with Mom

Chapter 3

I have my ice skating lesson this afternoon," said Gwynn the next day. She called out to Arne. "Is Mom taking me to skating?"

"No, honey. I'm taking you. Mom is busy," said Arne. "She'll probably meet us there if she has time." Mom had left the house before I got up. I was working on getting Flurry to jump on my back, since we weren't making progress with the chairlift. So far, I had gotten Flurry to stand next to me and eat treats off my back, but she was definitely puzzled by my request to climb up.

"I'm starting a new routine today," said Gwynn. She tilted her head back and raised her eyebrows.

"What's that look for?" I asked. I was on my hands and knees, trying to get Flurry to jump up by holding a treat in my left hand while Flurry was on the right.

"You know what it's for," said Gwynn. "Use your sister brain."

"You want me to come, too, to watch your new routine?"

I asked. Flurry crawled under me and tried to get the treat.

"Yes! You got it!" said Gwynn. She clapped her hands. "I need your positive thinking. Sister brain, still activated!"

Last winter, I had accidentally distracted Gwynn during her very first skating competition. She missed her jump because of me. Gwynn had forgiven me, but I still didn't feel as though I'd made things right. If she needed my support to get off to a good start, then I would be there.

🌲🌲🌲

Arne and I watched from the bleachers as Gwynn worked with her skating instructor, Ms. Margot. Gwynn did stretches along the short wall of the rink for a few minutes, putting one foot on top of the wall while the foot on the ice slid out, widening the split. Arne shuddered.

"I don't know how anyone can do that," he said. "I think I would break in half."

"I can do it, too," I told him. "Here, hold my foot and I'll show you."

Arne held my foot gingerly and made a face. "Doesn't that hurt?" he said as I stretched out.

"No! I love doing the splits. I used to be even more flexible when I was little. I wonder if I can still put my feet behind my head." Arne rolled his eyes and acted like his stomach hurt. It was kind of funny to gross out Arne. Not long ago, I wouldn't have teased Arne this way, but now we were closer, so it was okay.

"What if you split in two? What will I tell your mother?" said Arne. He set my foot down on the ground.

"You can tell her that she has three children instead of two," I said.

Arne made a noise, halfway between a laugh and a hiccup, and then he turned to the ice. "What do you think Ms. Margot is teaching Gwynn?" Ms. Margot was kicking out one leg while spreading her arms. Gwynn tried to copy her but lost her balance and sprawled on the ice. For a moment, I worried that Gwynn had hurt herself, but she popped back up and took a tiny half turn on the ice.

"What's happening? What did I miss?" Mom appeared next to me, squeezing me between Arne and herself. I grabbed Mom's hand and wrapped her arm more tightly around me.

"We're trying to figure out what Gwynn's next skill is," I said. Gwynn skated backward, dug her toe pick in, and threw her arms open before falling on her butt. Gwynn got up and talked to Ms. Margot. Then she skated over to us.

"I'm working on a split jump," said Gwynn. "But right now it feels like a splat jump. Every time I try to go up, I go splat!" She sighed. "They look so easy on television—like it's nothing at all!"

Surprises with Mom

"You'll get it," I said. "You just need more practice."

"I told Ms. Margot that I only want to do the skills that I'm already good at for my next routine, but she says no. She says I have to keep trying new things, even if I'm not good at them."

"She's right," I said. "What if you perform really well, but you don't win because the routine isn't difficult enough?" Ice skating judges give extra points for harder skills—that's how you get higher scores.

Gwynn's eyes widened. "Oh, I'd hate that!"

"Exactly," I said. "Besides, it's fun to try new things, right? That's why we do Five New Things every summer."

As Gwynn went to change out of her skates, Arne said, "Corinne knows what to say to keep Gwynn going."

"Corinne is a great big sister," said Mom. "And I think I want some time alone with the big sister. How about a mother-daughter afternoon?"

"Just the two of us?" I asked. "What about the store?" I couldn't believe it. I couldn't remember the last time I'd had time with just Mom. She was usually busy with the restaurant, and if she wasn't there, she was spending time with Gwynn or Arne.

"The store is covered. Molly's working this afternoon," said Mom. Molly was one of Mom's new employees. "Arne, can you take care of Gwynn?"

"Sure. I'll take Gwynn home," said Arne. "You two go enjoy your afternoon."

▲▲▲

Mom and I decided to walk to the bookstore, but we stopped to get ice cream first. We stood at the counter, looking at all the flavors. Mom handed me a dairy pill so I wouldn't get a stomachache from the ice cream. No one in my family, except Arne, can have ice cream without pills, because we're lactose intolerant.

"If Gwynn were here, she'd be reading all the flavors out loud," I said.

"She does seem to be going through a phase of listing things," said Mom. "The other day, she named all her favorite dim sum dishes." Mom looked at me. "I guess that bothers you, too, huh?"

"Sometimes," I admitted. I felt a little guilty, but I also felt better that Mom said *too.*

"It's just a phase," said Mom. "I remember when you were little, you went through a phase where you wanted to dunk everything in ketchup. Everything. Even, like, apples."

"I remember that! I couldn't understand why no one else liked apples and ketchup together," I said. "I thought it was cool that they were both red but tasted different."

Surprises with Mom

The girl behind the counter handed us our cones. Mom and I had both gone for really interesting flavors: chai for Mom and cilantro pineapple for me.

"Gwynn and Arne like the regular flavors," I said. "But we pick the unusual ones." I liked saying *we*, feeling close to Mom.

"That's right," said Mom. "It's one of the ways we're alike."

We walked slowly to the bookstore so we'd finish our ice cream before we got there. The bookstore used to be a house, and every space had books tucked into it, even under the staircase. One table featured cookbooks on barbecuing and making ice cream. Another table had books with purple covers.

The children's books were in their own room, so Mom said she'd meet me there after she looked around. There were lots of little kids in the room, squealing and dumping books on the floor while their parents stood around and chatted. A little boy in a T-shirt with a dump truck on it ran into my leg and shouted "Sowwy!" before running off in a different direction. The kids were cute, but they didn't make it easy to look at books.

I decided to go to the young adult section. That part of the store was separate from the kids' room, and it was quieter. Most of the book covers were kind of embarrassing,

Ice Cream

with lots of hand-holding and kissy-faces, but I found a book about making bedroom decorations that looked interesting.

"Make crafts that reflect your style and personality," read the back cover. "Create a space that makes you happy!"

A space that makes me happy? I loved the room that Gwynn and I shared—it looked like a bedroom in a TV makeover show. Gwynn and I talked at night, and we liked to make forts out of blankets and chairs. But sometimes it was hard to share a room with Gwynn. Lately, I just wanted a quiet space to myself.

When we had moved in with Arne, he'd wanted us to have our own rooms. I had offered to keep sharing with Gwynn so she wouldn't be scared about sleeping down-stairs from Mom. But Gwynn had grown up a lot since we moved in, and she didn't really need me anymore.

Maybe it was time to have my own room.

The more I thought about it, the more excited I got. I'd be a better big sister if I had my own room. I wouldn't get mad at Gwynn for doing her normal Gwynn things. I could invite my best friend, Cassidy, over for a sleepover, and we could have some private space. I could work with Flurry without being interrupted. I didn't want to hurt Gwynn's feelings. I just wanted my own space.

I tucked the book under my arm and went to look for Mom. This was the perfect time to mention the idea, when the two of us were alone. I'd even offer to give Gwynn the room that Arne had decorated and take the other one. Or the other way around. Gwynn could choose.

I peeked around the shelves for Mom. She wasn't in cookbooks or biographies, which were her two favorite kinds of books. I stood on my tiptoes to see if I could make out her hair, which was long and straight like mine. I spotted her across the store.

"Mom." I held the book out in front of me so she could see the cover. "I've been thinking, and I'm ready to move into the extra bedroom. Gwynn is old enough to have her own room, and I'd let her have first—"

I stopped when I saw the book in Mom's hand. The cover showed a woman with a rounded tummy. It was called *Your Baby in a Blended Family.*

For a second, I thought, *One of Mom's friends is having a baby!*

Then I thought, *We have a blended family.*

Mom must have seen the shocked look on my face, because she broke into a huge smile. "Corinne, I have some big news to share with you!"

Baby Blues

Chapter 4

"My mom is having a baby," I announced to Cassidy. I closed myself in the closet so Gwynn wouldn't interrupt. I said the words slowly and clearly because I was still getting used to the idea. "She just told me, and now she's telling Gwynn."

"WHAT?! Congratulations!" said Cassidy. "A baby! That's so exciting. I wish we had a baby." I heard Cassidy's mom say something. "Mom! Jake does not count! He's six and in kindergarten," said Cassidy. She lowered her voice. "My mom still thinks Jake is a baby."

Cassidy kept talking. "Do you remember what Gwynn smelled like when she was a baby? Babies have the best smell."

"They do," I agreed. I did remember sneaking sniffs of Gwynn's head when she was a baby. "As long as you stick to one end, anyway." I also remembered diapers.

"We can make things for the baby! Tiny little booties and blankies. Little hats. Oh, this will be so much fun!" Cassidy had taught herself how to crochet recently, so she liked having an excuse to make things. She had already made me a purple scarf. "Do you know if it's a boy or a girl?"

"Not yet," I said. "Mom said we'd know in a few weeks." There was something I knew already, though. "Mom told me about the baby after I asked to move into the spare bedroom. She said we're turning that room into a nursery."

"Ohhh," said Cassidy sympathetically. "That's too bad. But then again, I bet you'll get to hang out in a really cute nursery!"

"Maybe that part won't be so bad," I said. I hadn't even thought about how the nursery would look. "Arne will probably hire his designer to make the room really cute." I tried to sound positive, because that's how you were supposed to feel about babies. But I wished I had a way to tell Cassidy that I also felt something else. That when Mom told me she and Arne were having a baby, my stomach went kind of cold. I was supposed to be happy, and I was, but I had a lot of questions. Would Mom be okay? Would Arne feel differently about this baby because it was his? Would there still be time to work with Flurry and go on a training session with Kim?

"What are you doing in here?" Gwynn asked, opening the closet door. "Why don't you just talk in the room? Are you talking to Cassidy? HI, CASSIDY!" she yelled. "MOM IS HAVING A BABY!"

Cassidy yelled hi back, so I put my phone on speaker so I wouldn't get caught in the middle.

"Are you excited about being a big sister?" asked Cassidy.

"Oh yeah! I'm not a little sister anymore," said Gwynn. "I'm a big sister!"

"You're still a little sister," I pointed out. "You're *my* little sister."

"So I'm both," said Gwynn. She paused. "Well, that's weird."

"You'll be a middle child," said Cassidy. "Did you know that over half of the presidents of the United States have been middle children?"

"Oh," said Gwynn. "I like that."

"We'll call you POTUS," said Cassidy. "That stands for president of the United States."

"POTUS! POTUS! POTUS!" chanted Gwynn, jumping up and down.

I really wanted to talk to Cassidy alone. "Do you mind letting me finish my conversation?" I asked. "Privately?"

"This is POTUS's closet, too!" said Gwynn. "POTUS stays!" Cassidy laughed, but I was annoyed. I really wished I could have my own room.

🌲🌲

Corinne to the Rescue

A few weeks later Mom made pea soup for dinner, even though it was almost summer and soup is a winter food. Arne made pancakes to eat after the soup, which is a combination we'd never had before.

"I like these pancakes," said Gwynn. Arne had made Swedish-style pancakes, which were thinner than our typical breakfast pancakes. Arne showed us how to spread jam inside and fold them up.

"This is a tradition in Sweden," explained Arne. "On Thursdays, we have pea soup and pancakes."

"We have Taco Tuesday and Pea Soup Thursday," said Gwynn. "Pretty soon all the days of the week will be taken!" Mom and Arne laughed.

"If it's a tradition, why are we only doing it now?" I asked.

Arne shrugged. "Maybe because of the baby? I want to make sure he has Swedish and Chinese traditions," he said. Mom had found out yesterday that she was having a boy.

"He'll get plenty of both," said Mom. Her phone rang. Normally, no phones are allowed during dinner, but Mom was waiting for a call from my grandparents to tell them about the baby being a boy. She held the phone so we could all see. Gwynn and I waved at the tiny screen. "Hi, Po Po! Hi, Gong Gong!" My mom's parents live in New York. My grandparents waved back.

Baby Blues

"I wanted to tell you that you're getting . . . a grand-son!" said Mom.

A tiny cheer came from the phone. "A boy! Finally!" said Gong Gong.

"How are you feeling?" asked Po Po.

"I'm fine," said Mom.

"Girls, are you excited about your brother?" Gong Gong asked us.

"I'm going to be the baby's *er jie*," Gwynn told them eagerly. Second big sister. "And Cori gets to be the *da jie*!" Oldest big sister. My grandparents smiled. They always approved when we spoke Mandarin, even a little bit.

Normally I loved talking to my grandparents, but I didn't say much. All I could think of were those three words: *A boy! Finally!* It was as if Gwynn and I didn't count and this baby was the real thing.

After Mom hung up, I asked, "Why did they say, *A boy! Finally!* Like Gwynn and I were just practice babies?"

"That's not what your grandparents think, but some-times they just say things that people said when they were growing up. For a long time, boy babies were highly valued in China," Mom explained. "But times are changing. And they were just as excited when I told them about you and Gwynn," Mom said. "Really."

That didn't make me feel better. We were having pea

soup on Thursdays, which we never did before. And everyone seemed more excited about having a baby boy. Would there be any other surprises to go with the baby?

Cassidy, the Good Luck Charm

Chapter 5

A few weeks later, I invited Cassidy to go on a hike up Ajax with Flurry and me. Keeping Flurry fit was one of the things Kim had told me to do. I figured I could do that even if I couldn't get Flurry to jump on the chairlift or my back. This hike would be a special treat for Flurry. Dogs weren't allowed on the mountains in the winter unless they were official rescue dogs.

Cassidy and I packed a lunch, put on our hiking boots, and started up the Ute Trail. It was really steep, but Flurry didn't seem to mind the climb. She kept stopping to sniff trees.

"Can I pet your dog?" asked a woman hiking with a group. I nodded, and Flurry ended up getting pets from everyone. I swear she was smiling the whole time. Kim had said that Flurry needed to be well socialized, so I hoped this was a good sign.

Cassidy took a swig of water from her big stainless-steel

bottle. "I thought my mom was getting carried away when she told me to bring this, but I'm going to drink all of it," she said. Tiny beads of sweat were already glistening on her face.

"It's more dangerous to run out of water than food," I pointed out. "People can last longer without food than without water."

"I'd rather not run out of either," said Cassidy. "I like eating and drinking."

We talked about our favorite foods and our favorite drinks. Cassidy's favorite food was tacos. I had a hard time choosing between zongzi, sticky rice dumplings, and jiaozi, fried pork dumplings. We debated whether dessert should be included in the competition for favorite food, or if it should be a separate category. I said it should be included, but Cassidy insisted that dessert deserved its own category.

"And my favorite dessert is mint chocolate chip ice cream," said Cassidy, as if that decided everything. And which I already knew, because we were best friends.

We reached Ute Rock, which gave us an amazing view of Aspen. Cassidy took another drink of water. "I can't believe school is almost over," she said.

"Two more weeks and we're done!" I said. We turned and continued walking up the trail. "Then summer officially begins."

"You're definitely getting a head start on your Five New

Cassidy, the Good Luck Charm

Things," said Cassidy. "A baby should count as more than one thing."

"I mean, technically, the baby isn't going to be here over the summer," I said. "But, yeah, he's already changing things around." I was still thinking about Pea Soup Thursday and *A boy! Finally!*

"I was thinking we could—" Cassidy stopped. Flurry stood still, her nose twitching in the air.

"What's going on, girl?" I saw a flash of red-brown about fifty feet away, and a fluffy, white-tipped tail. "Oh, a fox!"

Flurry lunged and I pulled back on her harness just in time. "No, Flurry!" I said. She barked and pulled, yanking so hard that Cassidy grabbed her harness, too, to hold her back. The fox disappeared into the woods. Flurry stopped barking, but she continued to stare into the woods, growling.

"I've never seen Flurry like that," said Cassidy. "She's usually so gentle."

"Me neither," I said. My hands were sore from pulling back on her harness, and a little blood appeared where one of Flurry's metal tags had ripped open the side of my finger. I thought about Flurry getting into a fight with the fox and shuddered. She was bigger than the fox, but she still could've gotten hurt.

🌲

We stopped to eat by the side of the trail. We had packed our own lunches, plus food for Flurry. At home, I had wondered if we were packing too much. But now it seemed like we had barely enough, even with sandwiches, fruit, and cookies. "What do you think, Flurry? Do you have enough food?" Flurry gobbled up her lunch and slurped her water. "I think she wants more," I said to Cassidy.

"Agreed," said Cassidy. She closed her eyes and turned her face toward the sun. "I should have brought some lip balm," she said. "My lips are getting chapped."

"I wish I had a bandage," I said, examining the cut on my finger. It wasn't deep, but it would be nice to clean and cover it.

"We'll be better prepared next time," said Cassidy confidently.

We packed up the wrappers from our lunches, being sure not to leave any trash behind. "We can get a snack at Sundeck if we're still hungry when we get to the top," I told Cassidy. Arne had set up my ski pass with his credit card,

and I always carried it with me, so I could buy things at the restaurant.

"Well, we must be getting closer," said Cassidy. "Look! There's The Couch!"

If I hadn't been up the Ute Trail before, I might've started looking for a big upholstered sofa on the mountainside, but I knew The Couch was the nickname for a ski lift. It was easy to see why it was called The Couch. Each seat was wide enough for four people and had thick cushions. When it ran in the winter, the lift moved at a slow, easy pace. Because it was summer, though, the seats hung idle in the warm sun.

"That looks like a comfy place to sit!" I declared. We walked over to one of the seats that was low to the ground and sat down. The chair swayed slightly under our weight. Flurry sniffed the ground around us.

"Flurry deserves a comfy seat, too," said Cassidy.

"I don't think she likes chairlifts," I said. "She won't get on the one at home."

"But this one is different," said Cassidy. She called to Flurry. "C'mon girl!" She turned to me and asked, "What's the command you say?"

"Load up!" I said.

Flurry pricked up her ears and looked at us. I patted the seat next to me.

Cassidy, the Good Luck Charm

"Load up, Flurry!" Cassidy said. Then she put her thumb and index finger in the corners of her mouth and whistled. *Tweet!* I covered my ears.

Flurry broke into a smile and leaped onto the cushion next to me. She immediately lay down and put her head in my lap.

"She did it!" I said, astonished. "She won't do anything like this at home." Finally, I had something to tell Kim! "It's that whistle! Where did you learn to do that with your fingers?"

"I learned how to whistle from watching a video online," said Cassidy. "My regular whistle is so quiet that you can barely hear it." She pursed her lips to demonstrate. It was a very soft sound.

"You don't have that problem with the finger whistle!" I said, laughing. "I had to cover my ears! That must be why Flurry hopped up."

"Honestly, though, who wouldn't want to get on The Couch? It's so comfy." Cassidy leaned back against the cushion, sighing. "Maybe we should just stay here."

I was the opposite of relaxed, though. "You know what this means, don't you? Flurry finally did one of the things Kim asked for!" I grabbed Cassidy's arm. "You have to come camping with us! We're going to bring Flurry and try canoeing with her. We need you and your finger whistle.

Corinne to the Rescue

You're good luck!" I turned to Flurry. "We want Cassidy on this trip, don't we, girl?" Flurry smiled and put a paw on Cassidy, as if she agreed.

"If my mom says yes, I'm there," said Cassidy. "You know I love camping. Inventing new desserts. Making flower wreaths. Oh! I saw this thing where you can use sticks as a weaving loom."

I could already picture Cassidy camping with us. She'd make the trip perfect! "I have to ask Mom and Arne," I said. "But they have to say yes!"

Pregnancy Brain
Chapter 6

T o be honest," said Arne, "I've been wondering if this camping trip is a good idea."

"What?" I had just presented my argument for why Cassidy should come along, starting with Cassidy's good camping—and whistling—skills and ending with Flurry finally completing Kim's first requirement. It hadn't occurred to me that Arne might cancel the whole thing. "Why?"

"Your mom, she has been very sick with this pregnancy," said Arne. "I think camping would make her more uncomfortable."

"But I need to take Flurry canoeing," I reminded him. "It's part of her training."

Arne frowned a little. "We could do it another way, though, yes? Maybe canoeing with no camping."

"We always go camping," I said. "Every summer. It's a tradition."

"Well," said Arne. "You have to be reasonable, even

with traditions. The health of the baby is more important than dog training, right?" Arne acted like we were talking about dusting the furniture or putting forks on the correct side of the plate. But training Flurry to rescue people *was* important.

I studied Mom more closely. She looked mostly the same, except now her tummy was starting to stick out more. "Are you really sick?" I asked.

"Not sick-sick," said Mom. "I've just had some morning sickness."

"Except it doesn't just happen in the morning," said Arne. "Morning, afternoon, night. Anytime, she could go blah!" Arne made a face, opening his eyes wide and sticking out his tongue.

"Oh, it's not that big a deal," said Mom. "It's very normal, and it will go away soon. It's just hormones."

"I just don't want anything to happen to you or the baby," said Arne.

I remembered how scared Arne had been when I was lost on the mountain. He'd ridden the gondola up Ajax to look for me, even though he's afraid of heights. Now he was going to feel that kind of love for the baby, too. Or maybe, even more.

"The baby is fine," said Mom. "If anything, morning sickness means that the baby is doing well." She crossed her arms. "You're not going to keep me in bubble wrap just because I'm pregnant!"

"Ah," said Arne. "It just seems to me that camping is . . . inconvenient." Arne's first language is Swedish. I wasn't sure if he was using the word he meant to use.

"Inconvenient?" I asked.

"Yah, you know. Lots of fussing with this and that," said Arne, stirring his hand in the air.

"Arne, have you been camping before?" asked Gwynn. She'd been listening while she drew a picture. Arne shook his head. "Camping is awesome, not income-peanut."

"Inconvenient," I said, emphasizing the *v* sound.

Gwynn waved her hand dismissively. "Same, same." She turned to Arne. "It's so fun! We make food over a campfire and look at stars and sleep in a tent. And if you have to go to the bathroom in the middle of the night, you get to take a flashlight." When Gwynn mentioned the bathroom, Arne's forehead wrinkled. I jumped in with a diversion before he spent too much time thinking about that.

"Arne, this can count as one of our Five New Things!" I said. "Because we've never been camping together, or with Cassidy, or with Flurry! Have you been canoeing?"

"Oh, yes!" said Arne. He smiled. "I know canoeing. When I was a boy, we took boats out around the Stockholm *skärgården*."

Corinne to the Rescue

"The what?" asked Gwynn, which is what I was thinking.

"Oh, how do you say it? You know, so many islands? A big group of them?" Arne asked Mom.

"Um." Mom wrinkled her forehead. "Oh, I just had it. Pregnancy brain." Mom had been complaining about pregnancy brain a lot lately. It meant that she forgot things easily. It was definitely not like sister brain. Mom picked up her phone and tapped the screen. "Archipelago! That's what I was trying to think of."

"Yes! The Stockholm archipelago is very large, around thirty thousand islands, of all types. One of them even has a castle," said Arne.

"I didn't know there was a word for a group of islands." I savored the word. "Archipelago."

"Wait. Does that mean there are fancy words for other groups of things, like a bucket of water balloons? Or all your baby teeth after they come out? Or—"

I jumped in before Gwynn got too carried away with another list. "So, does that mean we can go camping? And Cassidy can come?"

Arne nodded, slowly. "Ah, yes, I suppose it does. We do need Five New Things." He wagged a finger at me. "But I expect a lot of help! I want your mother to be able to rest."

"Don't worry about a thing!" I promised. "Cassidy and I will do all the hard work."

Pregnancy Brain

🌲🌲🌲

After I had convinced Arne that we could still go
camping, I had a video call with Kim on Mom's laptop.
Mom stayed in the room but let me take care of the call.
I felt very grown-up talking to Kim like this. I was like
Arne on a business call!

"Hi, Corinne!" Kim waved. "How's it going over there?"

"Great!" I said. "I went hiking with my friend Cassidy,
and we got Flurry to load up on The Couch!"

Kim clapped her hands. "That's great! I like that you're
taking her on hikes, too. That will keep her in shape."

"That's what I was thinking," I told her.

"What about the other two tasks? Getting in a boat and
jumping on your back?" asked Kim.

"We're going camping soon," I said. "That's when we'll
try canoeing. And jumping on my back? We're, um, still
working on it." I didn't want to tell Kim that it hadn't been
going well so far.

"Just remember," said Kim, "you're really teaching
Flurry two things. She's figuring out how to *stand on* your
back, which feels really wobbly to her, and she's learning
to *jump onto* your back. So it helps to break it down. First,
you could encourage her to get on your back from a higher
surface, like a couch or bed."

Corinne to the Rescue

"Ohhhh!" My brain felt like fireworks were going off inside. Kim's suggestion made so much sense. Having a mentor was great! "I'll definitely try that. Thank you!"

"You're welcome," said Kim. She looked really pleased. "Take a video when she gets it! You'll want to have a record of her accomplishment."

I said I would, and we agreed to check in again after the camping trip. I really hoped I would be able to report that Flurry could ride in a boat and jump on my back.

I decided to take Kim's advice about breaking down the jumping skill into two parts. I got some treats and called Flurry up onto the sofa. Then I got on all fours on the floor and held one of the treats up in the air, so the only way she could get close to it was by stepping onto my back.

It was really awkward, being in a crawling position *and* holding out a treat *and* keeping an eye on Flurry. Maybe Kim wanted a video because I looked so funny! But then I felt the weight of one of Flurry's paws on my back, and then another. She was standing half on me, half on the sofa. That was something. I gave her the treat and she settled back onto the sofa.

"Good girl!" I praised her. "Now you're getting the idea."

The C+C Survival Kit Company

Chapter 7

To get Flurry ready for canoeing on the river, I had to teach her to sit in a canoe on the ground first. Luckily, one of our neighbors had one we could borrow. Mr. Harrington put the canoe in our front yard, and Cassidy came over to help.

I brought Flurry out on a leash and showed her the canoe. She cocked her head to one side, looking at it. "It's

a canoe, girl," I told her. She sniffed it, her breath echoing against the hard side of the boat.

I brought out a blanket that Flurry liked to sleep on and put it in the bottom of the boat. "Look, Flurry. Your nice bed! Want to get on your bed?"

Flurry looked at me, crouched down, and barked.

"I think she's saying, *You first!*" said Cassidy.

"That's a good point," I agreed. "Maybe if she sees me in it, she'll realize she's supposed to get in, too." I stepped into the boat and sat on the seat nearest the blanket. "Come on, girl!"

Flurry wagged her tail. She wasn't saying no exactly, but she wasn't quite ready to say yes.

"Maybe we should just put her in," said Cassidy. "Show her it's okay." She clucked her tongue at Flurry.

"No, she has to decide it's okay," I said. I had another idea. I went inside and brought out one of Flurry's favorite toys, a blue-and-pink rope. I dangled it in the air. Flurry's eyes gleamed.

"Get the rope, Flurry! Get the rope!" I waved it in front of her nose, and when Flurry tried to grab it, I snatched it away and ran to the opposite side of the boat. Flurry tried to run around the boat to get it, but every time she went one way, I went the opposite way.

"What's your plan?" asked Cassidy.

The C+C Survival Kit Company

"I'm kind of hoping she'll—" Before I could finish my sentence, Flurry did exactly what I hoped she'd do. She took a shortcut and jumped in and out of the canoe to get to me and the rope! She barked with the rope in her mouth, clearly pleased with herself.

We played around the canoe, getting Flurry comfortable with it. Next, we played hide-and-seek with the rope. I had Flurry sit and stay in one part of the yard, facing away from the canoe. Then I dragged the rope over the grass and hid it under the seat of the canoe. Flurry sniffed around the grass for a minute before picking up the scent of the rope. She leaped into the canoe and chewed on the rope contentedly while lying on her blanket.

Cassidy punched her arm into the air. "Success!"

"The real test is if she'll do this on the river," I said. "There's a big difference between dry land and moving water. We need to make sure she has lots of good thoughts about the canoe." I climbed into the canoe and petted Flurry. "The canoe is nice, huh, Flurry?" Flurry yawned and rolled over on her back!

"The canoe is just right for belly rubs," said Cassidy. She joined me in rubbing Flurry's tummy. "*Now* she'll think the canoe is really great! Isn't it, Flur?"

Mom came outside. "I've been watching you through the window," said Mom. "You were so patient, girls. Good job!"

"Now we have to make sure she can do it without the toy," I said.

We climbed out of the canoe so Flurry would get out, and then Cassidy and I stepped back in. This time, Flurry jumped in before I held out the rope toy.

"I think you've got it!" said Mom. "I'll make sure to order a life jacket for Flurry so it comes in time for the trip."

"Most dogs know how to swim," Cassidy pointed out.

"A life jacket isn't just for people, or dogs, who can't swim," Mom said. "If you get hurt or tired, it will protect you. A lot of people get in trouble because they don't realize how tiring it is to swim in a moving current."

"Gwynn hates wearing life jackets," I said. "She says it feels like she's stuck in a marshmallow."

"Ah! Marshmallows! That's what I forgot to put on the shopping list for the camping trip!" said Mom. "How can we go camping without marshmallows?" She shook her head. "Pregnancy brain!" Mom went back into the house.

"What do you want to do now?" I asked Cassidy.

"I have an idea," said Cassidy. "We could make a survival kit! Like, all the stuff we wish we had when we hiked up Ajax." Cassidy was always itching to make something.

"Great idea!" I said. "What should we put in it?"

We went inside and gathered things that might be useful: matches, safety pins, a tiny roll of duct tape. "We should put in some first aid supplies," said Cassidy. We poked around in the closet where Mom kept that kind of stuff and found some bandages and a little pouch of ointment. I grabbed a tube of cherry-flavored lip balm, remembering Cassidy complaining about her chapped lips.

"What can we use to hold all these things?" I wondered.

"Let's check your recycling bin," said Cassidy. We found an empty bottle of Mom's pregnancy vitamins. "It's perfect." The cap closed tightly, and everything fit inside. I found some bright pink paracord and wound it around the bottle.

"Now we won't lose it!" I said.

"We could make different kinds of survival kits for different situations," Cassidy said.

I thought about the day I had gotten lost on the mountain. "Like one with a whistle and food and hand-warmers. And a glow stick."

"How about one just for a bad day?" Cassidy asked. "It should have a funny comic strip . . ."

"A joke! Stickers! And glitter," I said.

"Chocolate! Gummy bears!" Cassidy said. "Oh wait, peppermint! I heard that smelling peppermint makes you feel better."

"I think we have some peppermint candies left over from Christmas," I said.

"The C and C Survival Kit Company," Cassidy said. We shook hands on it, like a real business deal.

I thought about the times that Cassidy had helped me get through a tough spot, like when my parents got into arguments. "Our motto could be, 'Friendship is the ultimate survival tool!'" I said.

An In-Tents Day!
Chapter 8

*R*emind me again," said Arne. "Why are we going to so much trouble to pack up everything but the kitchen sink to leave the house, instead of just staying home?" Arne smiled to show he was kidding, though the truck was really full. Cassidy, Gwynn, and I had sleeping bags tucked under our feet, and Flurry was sitting in my lap.

"You know what we didn't bring?" I asked.

Arne groaned. "The refrigerator?"

"Homework!" I said, and Cassidy and I high-fived. Our last day of school had been two days earlier, and I was already used to not having homework.

"Just wait," said Mom to Arne. "There's something about being outside, sleeping under the stars . . ."

". . . Missing my nice, soft bed!" teased Arne. He looked at us in the rearview mirror. "You all are going to turn me into a camper, huh?"

"You bet!" I said, though I wondered if Arne would want to go camping once the baby came. I couldn't remember seeing many babies when we'd gone camping in the past.

Soon we were out of Aspen, climbing into the mountains. Sunlight flashed between the trees.

"Is this where I turn?" asked Arne. "Check the map on my phone."

"Your phone's no good out here," Mom told him, smiling as she unfolded a map. "The signal is pretty nonexistent outside of Aspen. It's back to paper maps and face-to-face conversations."

"Oh no!" Arne pretended to be disappointed. "I guess I cannot do any work on this trip!"

"Nope! You have to have fun with us," I told him.

🌲

We got to the campground early in the afternoon. We showed Arne how to pick a spot that was nice and flat for the tent, and to move any rocks and sticks that might poke us through the bottom.

Arne watched with amazement as Gwynn, Cassidy, and I assembled the tent. "I can't believe you put that up yourselves," he said, as we made a neat row of five sleeping bags, plus a folded-up blanket for Flurry.

"The girls have had a lot of practice," said Mom.

"I told you Mom wouldn't have to do any work!" I reminded him. "Easy peasy."

An In-Tents Day!

"Now who's hungry? I packed lunch," said Mom.

"I am!" said Arne, rubbing his stomach. "I worked up an appetite watching the tent go up!" He carried the cooler to the picnic table that came with our campsite. Then he picked the cooler back up and peered more closely at the table. "There's dirt on the table," he said. "Actual dirt."

"That's because we're outside," I said. "There's dirt outdoors."

"That dirt won't hurt you," said Mom. She brushed the dirt off the table with her hand. "See? All better."

Arne shuddered. "I guess I am a city boy in some ways." He sat down gingerly. "But I can adapt." He looked at Mom hopefully. "Do we have wipes?"

"I don't think wipes would do much good on this old picnic table," said Mom. "But the sandwiches are wrapped in wax paper, so we can eat off that." She opened the cooler and handed out the food.

"My mom says that the average person eats six pounds of dirt in a lifetime," said Cassidy cheerfully. "She also says that dirt improves your immune system." Neither of those facts seemed to comfort Arne.

🌲🌲🌲

After lunch, we walked down to the water and had a rock-skipping contest. Cassidy and Arne tied at seven skips.

Corinne to the Rescue

Flurry dashed through the water, back and forth, carrying a ball we had brought with us. She shook her fur so the water droplets flew everywhere. Then we walked over to the general store to buy some firewood and ice cream. Arne bought a waterproof hiking map with lines all over it.

"Now this," he said, "is a map!" Arne was very excited. "When I was a young man, I worked on a project to make digital topography maps of the earth." He unfolded it on the picnic table so we could look at it carefully. "A topo map shows you the contours of the land. The closer the lines are together, the steeper the area is."

I pointed to a spot on the map. "This is where we are." I recognized the name of the campground. I squinted and tried to match the land around us to the map.

"And where's the bathroom? Oh! Over here!" Arne stuck his finger all the way over on the other side of the map. We all burst out laughing. We had picked our campsite because it was pretty, not convenient to the bathroom.

"It's not that far," Gwynn told him.

"It's not that close," said Arne. "We should have brought our own toilet!"

"We'll put it next to the fridge," I said. "Next time."

"Ach. Let's go for a walk," suggested Arne. "We can try out the map."

🌲🌲

An In-Tents Day!

I thought all of us would go, but Mom said she was going to take a nap in the tent. Part of me wanted to stay close to Mom, but she gently shooed us out of the tent.

"I know what will happen if you girls stay. First the wiggling, then the giggling. I won't get a moment's rest!" she said, smiling. This was another change in Mom—she got tired so easily.

That put Arne in charge. He smiled tentatively and said we would stick to the marked trails. He handed me the map, pointed to the trail, and asked us where we thought it would go.

"The lines get closer together," I said. "So it looks like we'll go uphill?"

"And the trail looks like it goes around a bump," said Cassidy. She traced her finger along the paper.

"What's that?" asked Gwynn. She pointed to a blue line.

"That's water," said Arne. "Probably a stream or a river. Do you know how you can tell which way the water is flowing?" When we didn't say anything, Arne gave us a clue. "Water can't flow uphill."

"Oh, okay!" I could see it now. I pointed to a number 13,000 on the map. "The elevation is higher here, so the water is flowing down to here." I pointed to a lower number, 10,800.

"That's right, Corinne," said Arne. "So, let's hike in and

see if our predictions are right."

Following the map made the hike a little slower, but I liked keeping track of where we were. The bump on the map turned out to be a huge rock formation that we had to walk around. The path did get steeper in the places where the lines got closer together. And we did find a stream, just where the map said one would be.

"Wouldn't it be great if we had a map for life?" said Cassidy. "Like, where the lines get closer together, you know that something hard is coming. And when they're far apart, things are normal. And maybe the blue lines are things to prepare for?" She pretended to read a map. "Uh-oh, lots of homework coming up!"

"Spelling Test Valley ahead," I said, joining in. "Easy words only!"

"But after that, there's Baby Brother River!" said Gwynn.

Arne laughed. "I think a baby brother is more like a mountain," he said. "Maybe a whole mountain range."

We followed the path downhill toward the river and came to a meadow. It felt like we had fallen into a painting.

Flurry leaped into a cluster of delicate purple and white flowers. "Look! Columbines!" I said. "And those are Queen Anne's lace and lupines." I pointed to bunches of white flowers with flat, lacy tops and tall stalks covered with

An In-Tents Day!

small purple flowers. But columbines were my favorite.

"The columbine is the official flower of Colorado," I told Gwynn. "I'll show you a trick. *Columbine* comes from the Latin word for 'dove.' Can you figure out why?"

Gwynn scrunched up her face. "Because some of the petals are white, like a dove?" Columbines come in different colors, but these flowers had five rounded white petals cupped inside five pointy purple petals.

"Nope!" I gently bent the stalk so Gwynn could see the underside of the flower. "Look now."

"Ohhh! The petals look like doves having a meeting!" said Gwynn. Each of the purple petals had a rounded tip that looked like the head, and the rest of the petal flowed out like the bird's body and tail. Flurry stuck her head between us, sniffing the flowers.

"Next you have to learn 'Where the Columbines Grow,'" said Cassidy. "It's one of the official songs of Colorado." Cassidy started singing the song, swinging her head back and forth for effect, her ponytail held in place by her favorite red, black, and yellow scrunchie. I joined in for the chorus.

Tis the land where the columbines grow,
Overlooking the plains far below,
While the cool summer breeze in the evergreen trees
Softly sings where the columbines grow.

"Groooooooow!" Cassidy and I bellowed, extending the last note.

Flurry began howling. *Awwwwwooooo!*

Gwynn pretended to cover her ears in agony. "The flowers are better than the song," she said.

"I myself prefer 'Rocky Mountain High,' which is the other official song of Colorado," said Cassidy.

Arne stood up and sighed happily. "What a beautiful place." He took a picture of Cassidy, Gwynn, and me with our arms around Flurry in the middle of the flowers.

An In-Tents Day!

"Blooms among flowers," said Arne, showing us the picture. "We should probably start heading back. I don't want your mother to worry."

"I wish we could wrap up this feeling and take it home with us," I said.

🌲🌲🌲

When we got back to the campsite, I peeked through the mesh door of the tent. Mom stretched and waved at me.

"Did you girls have a nice hike? Are you hungry? Should we start making dinner?" she asked.

"You sit," I said. "We'll take care of it."

Tonight's dinner was easy enough for Cassidy and me to fix: walking tacos. Instead of using taco shells, we added taco fixings to a snack-size bag of corn chips. I'd already helped Mom cook the meat at home, so we just needed to heat it up over the campfire.

"I made fire starters!" Cassidy announced. She poked around in her backpack and found them. She had stuffed empty toilet paper tubes with dryer lint and wrapped the tubes in wax paper, twisting the extra paper at each end. They looked like big pieces of candy.

Cassidy and I filled a bucket of water from the water pump and carried it to the fire ring in case we needed to put out the fire quickly. Then we showed Gwynn and Arne how to stack the twigs and sticks.

"It's like making a log cabin," said Gwynn. Arne watched and nodded.

"But, unlike a log cabin, you want lots of space between the sticks so the air can flow and keep the fire going," I said.

Cassidy added one of her fire starters to the small mound and asked Arne if it was okay to light it.

"Wait, Cassidy," I said. "You need to pull your hair back."

"Oh gosh!" Cassidy reached up and felt her hair. "My scrunchie must have fallen out during the hike. I didn't even notice."

"It was one of your favorites!" I said. She'd made the scrunchie herself.

Cassidy shrugged and then grabbed one of the long, thin sticks we were saving for the fire. She wound up her hair and jabbed in the stick. Now she had a bun.

With Arne supervising, I showed Gwynn how to swipe the match over the strike pad on the side of the matchbox. It took her a couple of tries, but finally a flame appeared.

"Ah!" Gwynn yelled, and dropped the match into the fire ring.

"Did it burn you?" I asked.

"No, I just didn't think it would work!" she said.

After a few more tries, we lit the wax paper on one of

An In-Tents Day!

Cassidy's fire starters and watched it catch. We had a fire!

Everyone clapped.

"Good job!" said Mom, coming out from the tent. "I knew I could count on you girls."

Banana Boats
Chapter 9

"*T*ime for dessert!" Cassidy and I announced after everyone had finished their walking tacos.

"Banana boats!" Mom put her hand on her forehead. "I bought the bananas and then forgot what they were for!"

"Pregnancy brain," Gwynn said.

"First we have tacos that walk, and now we have bananas that are boats?" asked Arne.

I showed Arne how to make a banana boat. I cut a banana down the middle so the skin opened like a wallet. Then I stuffed the space with yummies. Mom had brought chocolate chips, marshmallows, graham crackers, pretzels, and peanuts.

"How do you choose?" asked Arne.

"I like going for the s'mores combination," said Mom. "Chocolate, marshmallows, and smashed graham crackers."

"I firmly believe that more is better," said Cassidy, making sure to tuck something into every last space inside the banana peel.

Banana Boats

I chose pretzels and chocolate chips to make a sweet-and-salty combination. Gwynn alternated chocolate chips and marshmallows so they looked like teeth. Arne tried a little of everything, though not as much as Cassidy. "When I lived in Sweden, we had bananas on pizza."

"Bananas on pizza?!" Gwynn shouted.

"You have pineapple on pizza," said Arne. "Same idea."

It did not seem like the same idea at all to me, but I could see his point. We wrapped the bananas in aluminum foil and nestled them near the coals of the fire.

"Ahhh," said Arne. We sat around the fire and waited for the bananas to heat up. Mom and Arne rocked in two portable rocking chairs. The rest of us sat on logs. Flurry climbed into my lap. This was one of my favorite things about camping. Just hanging out and being together.

"This is the best," Cassidy sighed.

Corinne to the Rescue

The foil-wrapped bananas gave me an idea. "We should add aluminum foil to the survival kit," I said to Cassidy. "You can use it for a lot of things."

"Definitely!" She ripped off an extra piece and folded it. I got out the bottle and stuck the foil inside. Our survival kit looked pretty impressive!

Cassidy touched the banana boats and announced they were ready. We dug our spoons into the warm gooey centers. Flurry got a biscuit for her dessert.

"Why don't we make these at home?" asked Gwynn, licking her spoon between bites.

"It's nice to keep some things special, just for camping," said Mom.

"This is so good!" said Arne. He took a big bite and then leaned over to talk to Mom's tummy. "What about you, baby? Do you like all these goodies?"

"Oh!" Mom sat upright. "I think he does! He just kicked!" She grabbed Arne's hand and put it on her stomach. "Did you feel that?"

"I did!" Arne got a huge smile. "Oh my goodness. Oh my goodness." For a second, I thought Arne was going to cry. He got up from his chair and hugged Mom. "Girls, come here. This is amazing."

Gwynn went over, and Mom placed Gwynn's hand against her stomach. "Was that it? Does it hurt?" she asked.

Banana Boats

"No, no," said Mom. "Though the kicks will get stronger."

"How about you, Corinne? Or Cassidy? Do you want to feel?" asked Arne.

Cassidy shook her head shyly. "I remember when my mom was pregnant with Jake," said Cassidy. I couldn't blame Cassidy for feeling shy. Cassidy and my mom were close, but maybe not touch-Mom's-tummy close.

"I sort of remember you being pregnant with Gwynn and Gwynn kicking," I said, stroking Flurry's head.

"Do you want to come feel?" asked Mom. "You'll need to hurry."

Flurry got off my lap and I walked over to Mom. She put my hand on the side of her stomach and I felt a nudge. "There he is!" I said.

Mom leaned back. "Wow. First kick! I forgot how exciting that is." She tilted her head back and smiled.

"Maybe we should name the baby Banana Boat," said Gwynn.

"Banana Boat . . . Banana Boat," said Arne. He put his hand on his chin, pretending to think about it. "I think I like Banana Pizza better." Gwynn giggled.

"He'd have a lot of explaining to do at school," said Cassidy. "Poor ol' Banana Pizza."

"Actually, we have been thinking about names. Serious names," said Mom. "I like Samuel."

"And I was thinking Loo-veh," said Arne. "It's a Swedish name. And it's spelled L-O-V-E."

Were Mom and Arne seriously thinking of naming the baby Love? "Everyone will think his name is Love," I said, pronouncing it the normal way.

"That would not be the worst thing," said Arne. He was still really happy from feeling the baby kick. I stood up and started getting the washtubs ready for cleaning the few dirty dishes we'd made. I felt so confused. I was excited about the baby, but hearing that Arne wanted to name the baby Love made me feel a little uneasy. Did that mean that Arne was going to love the baby more than he loved us?

🌲🌲🌲

After we finished washing the dishes, we all walked down to the beach.

A woman stood next to a red canoe on the shore, looking up at the sky. "Hi, pup!" she said when she noticed Flurry. "Is she friendly?" I said yes, and she held her hand out for Flurry to smell and then petted her. She said her name was Lori and that she worked at the campground.

"What were you looking at up in the sky?" Gwynn asked.

"The Summer Triangle," said Lori. "Do you all know how to find it?" She crouched down to our eye level and pointed. "The Summer Triangle is made up of three bright stars: Deneb, Altair, and Vega."

"But I can see lots of stars!" said Gwynn.

"That's because it's a really clear night," said Lori. "You're seeing part of the Milky Way."

"We know about the Pleiades," I said, remembering the meteor shower we had watched with Dad over the winter.

"I love the story of the Pleiades, the Seven Sisters. I'm guessing you two are sisters," Lori said to Gwynn and me. Gwynn nodded, but I felt a little start. I wondered what people would think when they saw me and Gwynn with the baby. Would they guess we were related? How much would the baby look like us? Would the baby need dairy pills when he got older, like me, Gwynn, and Mom, or would he be able to go without them, like Arne?

"I'm also guessing you folks are one of my families going canoeing tomorrow," Lori said.

"Yep!" Cassidy said.

Lori nodded. "I'll be your ride to the canoe drop-off." Flurry pulled me toward the canoe on the beach. Maybe she remembered the fun we'd had with Mr. Harrington's canoe. "Do you like going on the water, pup?" Lori asked.

"We're going to find out tomorrow," I said. "We've been practicing on dry land." I let Flurry explore the canoe a little. Suddenly, Flurry leaped up and into the boat. She sat down by the front seat and looked at me as if to say, *Well?*

Lori burst out laughing. "I think you have your answer."

"Come on, Flurry. That's not our canoe," I said. I tugged on her leash. Flurry looked at me stubbornly and then lay down in the canoe. She really wanted to go for a ride, or maybe she was hoping for a belly rub.

"You might get some pretty fast canoeing tomorrow," Lori said. "We've gotten a lot of snowmelt."

"Hear that, Flurry? We're going to have a fun day in the canoe tomorrow," I said. "Now, out!" Hearing the command and my sterner tone, Flurry jumped out of the canoe and wagged her tail.

I was proud of how Flurry obeyed me. I hoped she would like the canoe just as much when it was on the water.

On the River
Chapter 10

The next morning, we walked to the camp office to board an old white van that was towing a trailer stacked with canoes. Another family was there, too. Lori popped out from the van. "Hey folks! Let's go!"

As the van bumped along the road, Lori told us what to expect. She had to shout over the roar of the engine. She was driving us to a point upriver where we could put our canoes in and paddle back down to the campground.

"You can stop and pull off anywhere you want along the river, as long as you're back to the campground by six. Let the person working in the general store know you made it back safely," she said.

"Look at that!" shouted the boy from the other family. A furry, golden-brown animal was sunning itself on a rock. "What is it? A beaver?"

"It's a marmot," said Lori. She slowed down the van so we could get a better look. "Isn't it cute? They're so interesting. They will cry and whistle to warn each other about potential predators. Some people call them whistle pigs."

Cassidy leaned against me. "Whistle pigs, banana pizza. This is a weekend of words that shouldn't go together, but do."

"Friend burrito," I said, coming up with my own mismatched words.

"Cheese socks," said Cassidy. We both burst out laughing.

Lori parked the van by a wide, sandy spot where it would be easy to get the canoes into the water. After she helped us unload the canoes and paddles, she gave us a safety talk. "If your canoe hits an obstacle, lean into it. Don't lean upstream—that makes it easier for your canoe to flip," she said. "If you do flip, stay calm. If you're in rough water, make sure your feet are facing downstream. You want to hit things with your feet, not your head. And keep your life vest on at all times!"

The other family took off quickly, since it was just two adults and one kid. They disappeared around the bend before we were done putting on our life jackets.

Despite her pregnancy brain, Mom had remembered to buy a life jacket for Flurry. It was a nice turquoise color with

On the River

a handle on the back. The jacket had pockets and loops for holding things, so I tucked Flurry's lunch and water bottle inside. "You can carry your own gear!" I told her. The life jacket reminded me of the vest she wore for playing rescue games in the snow. Maybe that's why Flurry didn't mind wearing the life jacket. Gwynn sure did, though.

"It's too tight!" whined Gwynn, wiggling around. "Can't you loosen it?"

"A little bit," said Mom. "But not too much. We don't want the jacket to float up over your head if you end up in the water." She reached around to adjust the buckles.

"I think I left my water bottle on the bus," said Arne. He sighed. "No matter, I think we still have enough water."

He squirted some sunscreen into his hand and applied it to his face. "Everyone, get some sunscreen on!"

"Can we hurry up?" I asked. "I'm getting hot." The river glistened temptingly. I was all set in my life jacket. It even had a pocket perfect for holding the survival kit!

"Just be patient, Corinne," said Mom. "You're the big sister. You should act like it."

"I hope no one here is a *badkruka*," Arne said. He was smiling, trying to lighten the mood.

"A bad . . . crouton?" asked Cassidy.

"*Kru-ka*," said Arne, more carefully. "A *badkruka* is someone who won't get in the water. A bath coward."

"Ha! That won't be me," said Cassidy. She pulled up her T-shirt to show that she was wearing her swimsuit underneath. "I'm prepared!"

"Me, too!" I said. I had also worn my swimsuit under my clothes. I liked canoeing, but I also liked getting into the river. "No *badkrukas*!" The sky was bright and clear, and it was already pretty warm.

"Very prepared," said Arne, nodding approvingly. "Good."

"Come on, Gwynn. You heard Lori. We have to wear it." I widened my eyes, teasing her. "You're not a *badkruka*, are you?"

"No! I'm a good kruka!" said Gwynn. "The best kruka!" She tugged on the strap to show the life jacket was secure. "Let's go!"

Mom said Gwynn would ride in the smaller canoe with Arne, and she would ride in the larger canoe with Cassidy, Flurry, and me.

"Wouldn't it make more sense for Mom to be in the canoe with Gwynn, since Gwynn is lighter and Mom won't have to paddle as hard?" I asked.

"Well, you're going to be doing most of the paddling!" said Arne. "Remember? You said you'd do all the hard work." He handed the paddles to Cassidy and me and pushed our canoe halfway into the water. I called to Flurry, but she didn't move until Cassidy did her finger whistle. *Tweet!* Flurry hopped into the canoe, making it wobble. She paused and looked back at the shore. Her tail twitched back and forth. That meant she was nervous. But she made it into the boat!

"I told you that you were good luck!" I said to Cassidy, relieved, as Arne pushed us the rest of the way in the water.

"I think it's the whistle," said Cassidy. "It's nice and loud."

"You'll have to teach it to me." I put my fingers in my mouth and tried to whistle. I made a noise halfway between a raspberry and a honk.

Flurry whined a little, tapping her paws up and down. "Flurry, down," I said. I petted her, trying to keep her calm. "See? It's nice here out on the water."

"Don't let her jump out," said Mom.

"I can't paddle and hold on to Flurry at the same time," I said. "But I think once she gets used to the movement of the boat, she'll calm down."

We started in a low spot, where cottonwood trees edged the water. A few deer watched us go by, their tails flicking. Flurry's ears and tail perked up as she stared back at them, but she didn't try to get out of the boat. We spotted an old house so run-down that we could see bits of sunlight coming through holes in the roof. I dropped my hand over the side of the canoe and let water run between my fingers. Flurry sighed and lowered herself into the hull, resting her chin on the edge of the canoe. She was doing it! She could ride in a canoe!

"Mission number two, complete!" I announced to Mom and Cassidy. "We have a boat-riding dog!" They cheered. "I can't wait to tell Kim when we get back!"

"Your hard work paid off," said Mom.

"I thought this would work, especially after Flurry begged to go for a ride last night," I said. "But it's good to know for sure."

We settled into a rhythm, paddling only when we needed to and taking in the sights. Lori was right—the river was high and fast. "Be sure to keep an eye out for logs," said Mom. "You might only see a branch poking out."

"Listen!" I said. The water sounded different here, almost like it was crashing. I spotted a small waterfall, splashing down from the mountain. I pointed it out to Arne and Gwynn so they could see. They smiled and nodded.

"Water fight!" Arne yelled.

A spray of water crossed in front of me. Arne had flicked his paddle at our boat! Gwynn was laughing.

"No fair!" Mom called. "We can't let them get away with that!"

Cassidy and I splashed water back at them. Flurry put

her paws on the edge of the canoe and barked. Arne got me with a good paddleful of water, but I didn't care.

"Ahhh," I said. "The water feels so good. Nice cool water on a summer day."

"No bad croutons here!" said Cassidy. She splashed Arne back.

"Or whistle pigs!" I added.

"Or cheese socks!" Cassidy and I couldn't stop laughing. Then Mom, Arne, and Gwynn started laughing because we were laughing so hard.

As the sun rose higher in the sky, we drifted down the river, sometimes playing and sometimes just letting the water carry us softly. Flurry was doing an amazing job in the canoe. At one point, she saw another deer and sat up.

"Hold on to her," said Arne. "We don't need her running off into the woods and getting lost."

"She wouldn't do that," I said. But I thought of the fox from the Ute Trail and grabbed the handle on Flurry's life jacket, just in case.

🌲🌲🌲

After a few hours, we steered our canoes over onto a flat beach to eat lunch and take a break.

"What did you pack for lunch?" I asked Arne. He had put himself in charge of lunch on the river.

Corinne to the Rescue

"Oh, it's a good one," said Arne. He tapped the cooler. "I brought a *smorgasbord*. So many goodies to enjoy."

"I can tell from the way you say smorgasbord that it's a Swedish word," Cassidy told Arne. "You say it with extra"—she waved her hand in the air—"enthusiasm."

Arne unpacked the cooler, proudly showing us the food he'd brought: pickled herring, smoked salmon, lunch meat, cheese and fruit, and a loaf of crusty bread.

I set out Flurry's water and lunch. While she ate, we nibbled on the different foods. Cassidy had never tasted pickled herring. She picked up a piece with the tips of her thumb and index finger and sniffed it. "It smells like onions," she announced.

"Try it," urged Arne. "Maybe on a slice of bread."

Cassidy took a tiny nibble. "Hey! It's not bad!" she said. She took another bite. "It's kind of sweet."

I preferred the smoked salmon and the cheese. I mushed together a couple of pieces of cheese and nibbled the cheese blob into an L shape. I showed it to Cassidy.

"Look! Cheese sock!"

Cassidy laughed and took bites out of her piece of herring until it looked like a person. Then she ripped out the soft part of the bread and rolled up the herring inside. "Friend burrito!"

It was the kind of day where we barely had to say two

words to make each other laugh.

After eating lunch and resting, we played in the water. We threw Flurry's ball into the river for her to retrieve and made lumpy castles in the rough sand. Mom and Arne leaned against each other on a tree stump, watching us. I wondered how long it would be before we could do this again, after the baby was born.

By the time we got back on the river, the sun had gotten hotter. The river was starting to narrow, with boulders closing in on either side. Our canoe picked up speed.

"We need to be careful around these rocks," said Mom. "I'll steer, but you girls need to provide the paddle power to help keep the canoe straight." I looked back and saw Mom take a long stroke on the left side of the canoe, pulling the paddle all the way back to the stern so that the canoe turned to the right, away from a cluster of rocks.

"Flurry, down," I commanded, so that Flurry didn't get hit by a paddle.

The river wasn't wide and gentle anymore. Obstacles loomed all around us. Half-submerged trees and huge boulders crowded into the waterway. Our canoe even scraped over a few rocks.

"Now paddle on the left," shouted Mom. "Not fast. Keep us straight."

Cassidy and I paddled. And paddled and paddled. We

couldn't stop or the canoe would start to go sideways. My arms were starting to ache. I looked back to check on Arne and Gwynn.

"Gwynn doesn't even have a paddle!" I said.

"Gwynn can't really do much with a paddle," said Mom. "She's too young, and she's light enough that Arne can power them both. Our boat, on the other hand, needs all of us to work together. Speaking of which, keep paddling!" Mom was trying to be cheerful, but I heard an edge in her voice.

Arne drew close to us. "Ahoy!" he said. "Are we having fun?" He was panting a little. I looked jealously at Gwynn. She didn't have to do anything, *and* she was eating apple slices.

"Why—" I started. It was the only word I got out before a huge jolt shot through the boat and everything turned upside down.

Disaster!

Chapter 11

I clawed for air. What was happening? Suddenly I popped up into the bright sunlight. I was in the river! I coughed, shooting water out of my nose and mouth. I flipped around so my feet were downstream like Lori told us, to take the brunt of anything I might run into.

Where was everyone? What had happened to the canoe? I twisted around, trying to get my bearings. I spotted Cassidy making her way to the shore. Flurry appeared in my vision. She was paddling, and the life jacket helped keep her afloat. I swam toward her and grabbed the handle. "It's okay, girl," I said. The whites of her eyes were showing—she looked terrified.

"Corinne! Swim for shore!" I spotted Mom, waving frantically and pointing to Cassidy. Behind her, I saw Arne holding on to Gwynn. The water wasn't that deep. Once in a while, I could even feel the rocky bottom of the river under my feet. It was the current that scared me. The water was pushing, rolling, and pulsing, threatening to sweep us down the river, into rocks, to who knew where. A branch shot past me, nearly hitting Flurry.

We have to get to the others. The scariest thought of all was getting separated. I kept one hand on Flurry's life jacket, and we worked together to swim to shore. I kicked hard while Flurry pulled us along with her paddling. Were we actually moving? I kept my eye on my family and Cassidy, willing to get us all to the same place. *Do not get swept away.*

When we got close enough, Cassidy grabbed my free hand. She gripped me so tightly that her fingernails dug into my palm. I didn't care. The sound of my own gasping filled my ears like wind from a storm. Flurry whined, and I realized that I still held her handle in my other hand. I let go and lowered myself to the ground as Mom, Arne, and Gwynn staggered onto the wet sand and sat down. Arne was crawling.

Disaster!

"Are you okay? Are you okay?" Mom stared at us through her wet hair, her eyes huge. We nodded.

I pointed at Arne's pants leg. "What about you, Arne?" Blood was seeping through the fabric, below the knee.

Arne touched the spot and winced. "Something hit me, but I was focused on getting Gwynn."

"What happened?" asked Cassidy. "One second everything was fine, and then . . ."

"I think you hit a log or something under the water," said Arne. "We didn't have time to stop, and our boat crashed into your boat. I saw you go in right before we went in, and I grabbed Gwynn just in time." Arne turned to Mom. "Is the baby . . . ?"

"I think the baby is okay. I didn't hit anything with my stomach." Mom started to say something else, then stopped and turned gray. She turned and threw up in a bush. "Do we have any water?" she asked weakly. But the cooler and the water bottles had tumbled into the river in the crash.

"Here," I said. I handed Flurry's bottle to Mom.

"It's better than nothing," said Mom. She dribbled the water into her mouth, rinsed, and spat.

Gwynn was crying, trying to get in Mom's lap, but Mom was in no shape to deal with her. I grabbed her in a hug. "It's okay, Gwynnie. We're all here. Calm down. Calm down." Gwynn gulped and tried to stop crying. "We're going to be okay." Flurry whined and licked Gwynn's face. I rocked side to side, patting Gwynn on the back. Her breathing slowly returned to normal.

"Where are the canoes?" I asked. I spotted one, over-turned and pushed against some rocks by the rushing water. The other canoe was gone.

"I don't want to get back in the canoe!" cried Gwynn, getting upset again. Flurry joined in the howling.

I shushed both of them. "It's okay, it's okay."

"We don't have any paddles, so we couldn't get back in the canoe if we wanted to," said Arne grimly. "Let's figure out what we do have and what we need to do next."

It didn't take long to check our supplies. Arne had the topo map folded in his shirt pocket. I had the survival kit tucked into my life jacket. Flurry had a few treats in hers. That was it.

Arne tried to stand up and then quickly sat back down, wincing. He rolled up his pants leg, revealing a gash with an ugly purple bruise starting to swell underneath. Mom took off her life jacket for Arne to sit on, and the rest of us stacked up our life jackets to elevate his leg. I took off the vest I was wearing over my T-shirt, and Mom used it as a bandage for Arne's leg to stop the bleeding.

Arne put his head in his hands. "Ayyy. What was I thinking? We should never have done this."

Disaster!

"We'll be okay," said Mom. "They're expecting us back by six. When we don't show up, Lori will look for us."

"You need something to drink before then," said Arne. "You just threw up. You need to stay hydrated."

Mom looked at the river. "We could . . ."

"No," said Arne firmly. "Who knows what diseases are in there?"

"At least I had Flurry's water," said Mom.

"You need more," said Arne.

"Go find some sticks," I told Gwynn. We needed sticks, but more importantly, Gwynn needed a job to distract her. Gwynn jumped up and started gathering branches. "Don't go too far. There should be plenty on the beach." I started digging a shallow hole in the sand with my hands. "We can start a fire in this sand pit. We can drink the river water if we boil it first."

"That's a good idea," said Arne. "Just be careful."

Gwynn returned with an armload of sticks and branches, and we arranged them in the hole, putting the smallest ones at the bottom. We got lucky—they caught fire easily with a match from the survival kit. The fire was not the problem.

"You can't boil water in a plastic bottle!" said Mom. "The bottle will melt."

I was stumped, but Cassidy wasn't. "Don't doubt the

Corinne to the Rescue

C and C Survival Kit!" said Cassidy, pulling out the rectangle of aluminum foil. "Good thing we brought the heavy-duty foil." Cassidy carefully unfolded and refolded it to make a double-layered square. "Remember how we used to make paper cups in school?" she asked. She folded the square, corner to corner, to make a triangle. Then she folded the two pointiest ends inward to form a pentagon, gently turned down the two layers of the top corner in opposite directions, and pushed open the sides to form a cup.

"You did it!" I said, amazed.

"Now we just need some sticks to hold the cup over the fire," said Cassidy.

The foil blackened where the flames touched it, but the cup held together while the water came to a boil. After the water cooled, we passed around the cup and each took a drink. The water tasted good, but everyone was careful to take tiny sips to make sure Mom got the most.

"Can we do it again?" asked Gwynn when the cup was empty.

"The foil probably won't hold up a second time," said Cassidy.

"Just try to be still," said Mom. She closed her eyes and tilted her head back. "Don't do things that make you thirsty. Maybe we can take a nap."

Disaster!

"When is it going to be six?" asked Gwynn. No one answered. The sun was high in the sky, beating down on us.

I asked Arne for his map and spread it out on a rock. "Do you want me to show you where we are?" asked Arne. He shifted his weight and grimaced. His leg really hurt.

"I can figure it out," I told him. Cassidy looked at the map with me. "Here's the river, and here's the campground," I said. Arne had marked our campsite with a neat red X. "Where do you think we are?" I had an idea, but I wanted to see if Cassidy would come up with the same location before I said anything.

Cassidy traced her finger on the map. "Remember there was a sharp turn in the river before we stopped for lunch? I think that's here." She pointed to a bend in the river on the map. "And then there was that really pointy cliff, which looks like it would be here. So I think we're here?" She touched the map, right about where I thought we were. Bingo.

"Look," I said. "We can hike to the campground if we stay next to the river." I looked at the scale on the map. "I think it's about three miles. We can cut in here and get to the trail we took yesterday. That will get us to the camp office even faster."

"My mom says we walk about a mile in fifteen or twenty minutes. Maybe we'd be slower because we won't be on flat ground," said Cassidy. "But still, we could get help a lot sooner than six o'clock."

When we told Mom and Arne our idea, they both looked doubtful. "I appreciate that you want to help," said Arne. "But . . ."

"It doesn't seem safe," said Mom. "What if . . . ?" I knew she was thinking of when I'd gotten lost on the mountain, looking for the sister shrine Gwynn and I had made.

"This is different," I said. "We won't get lost. We have a map. It's daytime. And we'll be together."

"We just need to follow the river for the most part," said Cassidy. She showed them on the map. "See? We can be back to the campground in an hour, maybe a little bit more."

"I should go," said Mom.

"No, you need to rest," I said. "We don't have more water, and you can't risk getting more dehydrated."

"She's right," said Arne reluctantly. "It's hot. The girls can handle the heat, but you've already been sick once . . ."

I had one more argument. "Lori said if we aren't back by six, they'll look for us. But that means that they'll *start* at six. Who knows how long it will take them to find us? We can show them where you are. We'll take Flurry, too," I said. That seemed to decide it for Mom and Arne.

I turned to Gwynn. "You need to stay here and take care of Mom and Arne." Gwynn nodded solemnly. I didn't tell Gwynn the real reason: Cassidy and I could go faster without her.

"Okay," said Mom. "But if you become unsure of where you are, stay by the river, okay? Don't go into the woods. If Lori finds us first, we're going to tell them to look for you by the river."

Into the Wild

Chapter 12

*T*he hardest part about leaving was saying good-bye. Gwynn kept calling out to us as we hiked farther and farther down the river.

"See you soon!" Gwynn yelled.

"We'll be back in a little while!" I shouted back.

"Be careful!"

"Definitely!"

"Send me a sister brain when you get there!"

I tried to pretend that we were just going for a walk, but Gwynn's comments nearly did me in. I swallowed hard so she wouldn't hear the worry in my voice when I yelled back one last time, "Sister brain activated!"

Eventually, Gwynn's voice faded into the roar of the river, and then my family disappeared, out of sight. I could still see the thin column of smoke rising from the fire, but then that vanished, too. We were really doing this. For a few moments, all I could hear was the thud of our footsteps and the jangling of Flurry's collar.

Cassidy grabbed my hand. "We can do this," she said.

"We have the survival kit," I said, patting the pocket in Flurry's jacket where I'd stashed it. I couldn't believe that we had actually needed it. "And each other." I was so glad Cassidy was there.

"It's only a few miles. We went farther on the Ute Trail, and that's way steeper."

I gulped and nodded. "Only a few miles," I repeated. Only a few miles until we could get help. A stone caught the edge of my sandal and I tripped. Cassidy helped me up. Our shoes were meant for being on the water, not walking in the woods.

"We need walking sticks," Cassidy decided. We looked around for sticks that could do the job. Cassidy reached for a gray branch on the ground, but I pulled her back.

"Poison ivy!" I warned. "Leaves of three, let them be."

Cassidy took a step back. "Thanks for the save. That would have been bad."

"Well, it didn't happen," I said. "We just have to be careful."

"Should we check the map?" asked Cassidy.

"Sure." I pulled it from my pocket. According to the map, the river was going to widen soon, but we hadn't reached that point yet. The campground was still a long way away. We walked into a shady part of the riverbank, and I began to shiver. Between the shade and my damp clothes, it was easy to feel chilly, even on a hot day.

"We should sing," I suggested. "I always feel warmer when I sing." We sang "Where the Columbines Grow" and then "Rocky Mountain High."

"Do you know any more songs?" I asked Cassidy.

"We could sing Christmas carols," suggested Cassidy.

"In the middle of summer?" I gave it some thought. "We could change 'Jingle Bells' to 'Maroon Bells.'" I laughed. The Maroon Bells are two famous mountain peaks not far from Aspen.

"Ma-roon Bells, Ma-roon Bells, pho-to-graphed all dayyyyy!" sang Cassidy.

"Don't you want to take a hike, ride a bike, or play? Hey!" I added. Flurry wagged her tail and barked.

"What's another song?" asked Cassidy. "You should really know more songs."

"Why do *I* need to know more songs?" I asked. "Why don't you?"

"You're the one getting a baby brother," said Cassidy. "You're supposed to sing to the baby."

"Evvvvverything is about the baby," I said, half joking.

Flurry ran ahead of us and returned with a long stick. She dropped it at my feet. "Did you bring me a walking stick?" I asked her. It was actually a good stick—nice and smooth and just the right height and weight. I gave it to Cassidy to use. She started singing "Heigh-Ho" from *Snow White*, thumping the stick as we walked.

Singing helped pass the time. When we ran out of songs, we talked about movies and TV shows. That led to a contest to see how many names we could remember from Star Wars, which was Cassidy's favorite. "If only Gwynn were here," I joked. "She could probably list them all."

"Speaking of names, I know you weren't crazy about it, but I liked the name Love," she said. "It's sweet. And people would figure out how to say it the right way."

"Yeah, yeah, yeah," I said, hoping that we could talk about something else.

"You really don't like it?" said Cassidy. "Even if people say it right?"

"I can see it now," I said, holding up my hands. "The Christmas card with Corinne, Gwynn, and Love. Hey everyone, guess which kid we *love* the best?" My voice cracked on the word *best*.

Cassidy laughed and then stopped. "Oh wait—you're serious?"

"I'm not," I said, too quickly.

Cassidy stopped walking and looked at me. "Corinne Mei-Ling Tan. Your mom and Arne love you. You know that, right? Like, they're crazy about you. Heck, they did this trip basically because you needed to take Flurry canoe-ing." At hearing her name, Flurry looked back at us.

"They did," I admitted. "Though we always go camping in the summer." Actually, just saying out loud the thoughts that had been stirring around in my head made them seem less awful. "Maybe it's just that life will change. Will Mom and Arne still have time to help me with Flurry after the baby is born? And Arne's never had a baby before. Will he start acting different?"

Cassidy laughed. "That's pretty funny, thinking that you have more experience with babies than Arne. You'll have to show him the ropes!"

I laughed. I hadn't thought of it that way. I could be kind of like a mentor to Arne, just like Kim was a mentor to me. "I'll make sure he gets plenty of practice with the stinky diapers!"

We checked the map again. We were over halfway there, maybe two-thirds. Flurry dug around and brought me a twig.

"It's a little short for a walking stick," I told her. "But we don't have much farther to go!" I wondered how Mom, Arne, and Gwynn were doing. The baby, too. I hoped they were okay. It wouldn't be too much longer now. I picked up my pace.

Rockslide!

Chapter 13

As we rounded a bend in the river, a huge pile of rocks loomed over us. It looked like an angry giant had shaken the earth like a snow globe, except it had scattered giant boulders instead of snowflakes.

"Oh no!" I pulled out the map to double check. The map showed this area as being low and flat, at the bottom of a hill. Instead, piles of rocks blocked our way, spilling over the riverbank and into the river.

Corinne to the Rescue

"It's a rockslide," said Cassidy. "My family ran into one on the way back from my grandparents' house one year. It took us forever to get home because we had to backtrack and go all the way around. And remember Lori said there's been a lot of snowmelt? That makes rockslides more likely."

Some of the rocks were as big as cars, stacked up and teetering on each other. The force of the rockslide had taken out whole trees, which stuck out like toothpicks between the rocks. Even standing on tiptoe, I couldn't see where the rockslide began. It seemed to go on forever, up the hill and into the forest.

"What should we do now?" I said, half to myself, half to Cassidy.

"We promised your mom we would stay next to the river until we got to the trail that leads back to camp," said Cassidy. "I think we should stay put and wait. You always said that's what saved you on the mountain."

I thought about Mom and about Arne. Even Gwynn was probably thirsty now. "But we're not lost. We know where we're going. We just need to follow the map."

"But this isn't on the map. Who knows what else is covered by rocks now?" Cassidy sounded tired. "I feel like our only options are to stay put or go back."

I wasn't crazy about going back. We were so close to the

Rockslide!

campground, if we could only reach the trail. It would take a long time to get back to Mom, Arne, and Gwynn.

"Maybe we could go over," I said.

"Over that?" said Cassidy. "Not without a ladder!"

It wasn't like Cassidy to be negative, so her tone scared me a little. The rocks were dauntingly high, with no places to put our hands or feet. And there was always the risk of falling, even if we could get started.

A flash of purple caught my eye. I looked down and saw a tiny columbine poking out between two rocks. It seemed like an impossible place for a flower to grow, but there it was. This was a time to believe in the slightly impossible.

"Look," I said to Cassidy. "We're tired, but we're so close. It's important not to lose hope right now." I'd learned that from getting lost on Ajax. "We have to stay positive. Let's assume there's a way to get over safely and look for it. We can do this if we work together."

Cassidy closed her eyes, drew a deep breath, and exhaled. For a moment she didn't say anything. Then she looked me in the eye and said two words. "Cheese socks."

"Let's do this!" We hugged, trying to give each other courage.

We looked for a good place to start our climb and tested a few of the rocks with our hands. The problem was that the small rocks wobbled too much, and the big rocks were impossible to climb. We kept looking until we found one that wasn't as tall as the others. Cassidy was able to put her hands on top of the boulder. She tried to scramble to the top, but she fell back down. "It's still too high," she said. "And there's nothing to grab on to."

I studied the rock. "Here." I laced my fingers together. "Put your foot here. You can jump, and I'll lift at the same time." We counted to three, and then I lifted Cassidy as she stepped into the stirrup I'd made with my hands. She grunted and kicked her way up the rock. Then she turned on her perch, panting. "We did it!" said Cassidy. I handed her the walking stick. She reached down for my hand.

"Now you," she said.

"Wait. What about Flurry?" Flurry was a pretty good jumper, but she definitely couldn't jump that high. If I went up first, Flurry would get left behind. "Flurry needs to go next," I said. "C'mon, girl." I started to lift her by the handle on her life jacket but stopped. My arms weren't strong enough to lift her over my head. Flurry wiggled and whined, and I set her back down.

Cassidy put her hands on her hips and looked down at us. "Too bad you can't give her a boost like you just did for me," she said. "Should I come back down?"

"Not yet." Cassidy's comment had given me an idea. "I can't do it the same way I helped you, but I wonder . . ."

Rockslide!

I stood in front of the rock and bent over, making my back flat. "Call Flurry," I said.

"Flurry!" Cassidy called. Flurry cocked her head and looked at me, puzzled. I patted my back awkwardly. "Come on, Flurry!"

Flurry looked away, distracted by a bird chirping in a tree. Desperation washed over me. Maybe Flurry had forgotten about getting on my back. "Call her again," I told Cassidy. "Use your whistle!"

I bent over as Cassidy let out a loud *Tweet!* Flurry jerked her head toward Cassidy, then took a running start and leaped onto me. For a moment, she paused, all four feet on my back. Cassidy whistled again, and I felt Flurry push off me, bounding onto the rock next to Cassidy.

I stood up and threw my arms in the air. "She did it!"

"She sure did!" said Cassidy, petting Flurry. "I know I didn't look that cool when I did it."

"I mean, she also jumped on my back! That's the last one of Kim's requirements. Good job, Flurry!" Flurry turned around, as if ready to jump back down.

"No, Flurry! Stay there!" I held up my hand, palm facing Flurry. She backed away from the edge. Flurry and Cassidy looked down at me from the rock. Who was going to be my booster?

"Now it's your turn," said Cassidy. She reached her

hand down. Our hands could barely touch. I jumped up and grabbed her wrists for a stronger grip, but Cassidy wasn't strong enough to pull me the rest of the way. My feet scrabbled against the rock, trying to find a crack or a bump I could push against.

"Let me hold on to one wrist instead of two," Cassidy said. "That way you can stay closer to the rock. Try to find a foothold so you can use your leg power."

That made sense. We'd gone to birthday parties at the rock-climbing gym, and they always told us to keep one hip close to the wall. We reset. Cassidy used both hands to grip my left wrist while I spread out against the rock, feeling for places to grip. I found a spot for two fingers and held on. Now I just needed a toehold.

"I'm afraid I'm going to pull you down," I panted. I was feeling around blindly with my right foot. My arms were getting tired.

"No, no, you'll be okay," said Cassidy. "I've got you."

I grunted and reached my foot higher, still searching. There it was! A tiny bump. "I've got something." I tensed up my muscles and began to push up. It was so much weight on a tiny ledge. Would it hold?

"You've got this," coaxed Cassidy.

"I'm going to slip," I said. "Let go."

"You're not falling," said Cassidy, her voice tight with

Rockslide!

determination. "This is the way. You just have to do it."
I felt something wet grab my sleeve and pull. It was Flurry!
Now I couldn't let go. I closed my eyes and focused on
pushing up with my leg and pulling with my arm. My leg
was shaking from the strain. Up! Up! Up! Cassidy's grip
relaxed as I heaved myself on top of the rock. I had made it.

The first thing I saw when I opened my eyes was
Cassidy and Flurry smiling at me. The second thing I saw
was rocks. Big rocks, little rocks, flat rocks, rocks that could
start falling again and sweep us away.

I rolled onto my back and gave myself a minute to
recover. Getting up on the rock pile was just the beginning,
not the end.

"Step one down," said Cassidy. "Now steps two
through a million to go."

With every move, rocks wobbled and slid. "One step
at a time, one step at a time," Cassidy and I chanted. Our
steps were tiny. Flurry went faster, being on four feet.
Cassidy and I looked at each other.

"Why are we on two feet?" asked Cassidy.

"Beats me," I said. We dropped down to our hands and
feet. Much faster!

"How do we know that we're not going in a new direction?" asked Cassidy. We couldn't see the river now that we
were on all fours, though we could hear it.

Corinne to the Rescue

"We have the map," I said. "If we get off track, we'll figure it out."

Going over the rockslide took a different kind of effort. We had to constantly figure out which way to go, and even on all fours, we had to be careful.

Suddenly, Flurry stopped and growled.

Cassidy also stopped. "Cori, look," she said under her breath.

I followed her gaze up the rockslide. A yellow mountain lion stared down at us from a rock, its ears pinned back. The animal opened its mouth, exposing sharp white fangs. It made a noise halfway between a hiss and a scream.

My mouth went dry. The mountain lion was huge. Flurry tensed, ready to spring up the hill. I grabbed her life jacket handle with one hand, keeping an eye on the mountain lion the whole time.

"What do we do?" whispered Cassidy.

"We've got to act big and keep eye contact," I said in a low voice. "And we've got to get some distance between us. Now."

We scrabbled backward, trying not to trip on the rocks. The mountain lion bounded down from its ledge, getting so close to us that I could make out its whiskers.

I picked up a rock and threw it. "AAAAAH! START SCREAMING!" I shouted to Cassidy.

Rockslide!

Cassidy started screaming, too. "GO AWAY, CAT! GO AWAY!"

Flurry barked and howled and pulled on my arm. I tightened my grip on her handle. If I let go of Flurry, the mountain lion would kill her for sure.

"MAKE YOURSELF LOOK BIG!" I was still holding on to Flurry, but I raised my free hand in the air. Cassidy waved her walking stick.

"GET OUT OF HERE! GO! GO!" Cassidy yelled.

The mountain lion took a step back, hissing at us. I pitched another rock toward it while holding on to Flurry. The rock bounced near its feet, and the mountain lion took a step back.

Cassidy banged her walking stick against a fallen tree. *CRACK! CRACK! CRACK!* "GIT! GIT!" That was enough. The mountain lion backed away, keeping an eye on us. Then it ran back up the hill and disappeared over the rocks.

We kept screaming for another minute, just to make sure it was gone, really gone. Then we stopped. Cassidy lowered her stick, and without saying a word, we collapsed in a hug. My ears were still ringing with all of our screams.

"That was crazy," said Cassidy.

"I was terrified that Flurry would attack the mountain lion to protect us," I said. I held up my hand. My palm was criss-crossed with red lines from gripping the handle on Flurry's

life jacket so tightly. I unwound the pink paracord from the survival kit and threaded it through Flurry's life jacket handle. I tied the ends together so I had a loop to hold. "I think I'd feel better if she stayed leashed."

"We have to be close to camp by now, right?" asked Cassidy. We pulled out the map and looked and looked, but I couldn't tell where we were.

"We just have to keep going," I said.

I couldn't wait to get off the rock pile, away from the mountain lion, and onto solid land. Step, pause. Step, pause. I stepped on what looked like a stable, flat rock, but it moved under my weight. The rock slid down the long slope, triggering other smaller rocks to fall, too. A sound like thunder, heavy and rolling, began to grow. During an avalanche, you're supposed to grab on to a boulder or a tree to stay in one spot. But what should you do if the rocks and trees aren't attached to the ground?

"Look out!" I cried. Rocks were tumbling below us, and I worried the ones we were standing on would start to slip, too. Cassidy was uphill from me. Flurry leaped higher, closer to Cassidy. The cascade of boulders seemed to reach up, grabbing more to take with it. I forced myself to take a few quick steps, away from the retreating rocks. Gradually, the rolling and thundering stopped. I sat down on a sturdy rock, trying to catch my breath. Cassidy sat down next to me. I wanted to cry, but I was afraid that would scare Cassidy. I took a few deep breaths. *Don't give up.*

"Let's wait," said Cassidy. "Make sure it's really over."

"Yeah." I really didn't want to move. It seemed like we were safe here, sitting, with nothing moving. Then I remembered Mom, Arne, and Gwynn. They were depending on us.

"Let's get crawling," I said, trying to joke.

"We can crab-walk for a little change of pace," said Cassidy. We scuttled on our hands and feet, with our faces up and turned toward the sun.

"It's different, but more awkward," I said. "Especially while holding a leash." I stood up and stretched. A flash of green caught my eye. "Is that a meadow?" I wondered aloud. We had been working our way up the rockslide, but we'd had to zigzag across the rocks. Maybe we had changed direction. But I could still hear the river.

We crawled to the far side of the rockslide, where there were more steep rocks to climb down. But after everything we'd been through, getting down seemed easy, especially with solid ground in sight.

"You don't think the river split, do you?" asked Cassidy. "Maybe we've taken a branch?"

"I don't think so." I took out the map and studied it. "The map doesn't show a split. This kind of looks like where we hiked yesterday, but I don't see the trail any-where. If it is the same place, we're close." I couldn't decide if I just *wanted* this place to be what we were looking for, or if it really was. "The river is still on our left." My legs were starting to ache, but I tried to keep my voice cheer-ful and encouraging. "I think we'll reorient ourselves in a minute."

"I really want a drink of water," said Cassidy.

"We can get water from the pump back at camp," I said. It really did look a lot like the wildflower meadow we hiked through yesterday, but maybe it was a different one. I turned around, trying to match the landscape to the map. Flurry headed into some brush. "No, Flurry," I said, pulling back on her makeshift leash. She pulled again, harder, her nose to the ground. I saw a flash of red, black, and yellow, and my heart pounded.

"Get away from there," I said. "We don't need to go that way." Coral snakes were reddish, black, and yellow. I'd never seen one in Colorado, but I knew they were poisonous.

Flurry whined and yanked on the leash, breaking loose from my grip. "Flurry, NO!"

Flurry ran straight toward the snake and pounced on it with her front paws. "She's going after a snake!" I shouted at Cassidy. Flurry was going to get bitten for sure. I ran over and braced myself for Flurry's screams of pain.

Rockslide!

But Flurry just looked at us and wagged her tail. She was fine!

That's when I realized it wasn't a snake at all. "It's . . . a scrunchie?"

"A what?" Cassidy started laughing. She took a look. "Wait! It's my scrunchie! The one I lost yesterday. That means we *are* in the same field as yesterday. We're close to camp!" She picked up the scrunchie and put it in her hair.

"Look!" I shouted. "There's the trail! We just couldn't see it behind the brush. That trail should take us back!" I enveloped Cassidy and Flurry in a hug. "We're going to make it! Good job, Flurry!" I doubled up the leash and shook it at her, offering her a chance to play as a reward. Good girl!" Flurry grabbed it and pulled.

We tugged back and forth for a few seconds but then Flurry dropped the leash. I think she wanted to get back as much as I did!

We walked faster. The landscape became more familiar. When we saw the camp flagpole through the trees, we ran the rest of the way. We had made it. The first person we saw was Lori. She was in the parking area near the trail-head, talking on her walkie-talkie. When she saw us, she hurried over.

"Corinne? Cassidy? I didn't see you guys come ashore," Lori said. Her expression turned from relaxed to urgent as we told her what had happened. We showed her on the map where we had left Mom, Arne, and Gwynn.

"You girls did a great job making a plan and keeping your cool," said Lori. "I'm going to radio for help." She spoke into her walkie-talkie and took out some water bottles from the van. Cassidy and I split one, and Cassidy made a bowl with her hands for Flurry to drink, too.

A few minutes later, we were in a van with some other camp staffers, going to get Mom, Gwynn, and Arne.

Who Rescued Who?

Chapter 14

L ori took a logging road that brought us close to the spot where we'd left Mom, Arne, and Gwynn. Soon we spotted the smoke from the fire that we had started for boiling water. As we hiked over the ridge, Gwynn looked up at us and screamed. We hurried down to them, and I handed Gwynn a water bottle. She drank it greedily.

Lori brought out a first aid kit and checked Arne over. "We're going to splint your leg and carry you back to the van," she said. "And then I think we should get you to the ER for X-rays." She handed another water bottle to Mom. "How about you? Are you feeling okay?" She eyed Mom's stomach.

Mom nodded, but she polished off the bottle of water in a few gulps. She hugged Cassidy and me. "You girls are my heroes," she said. "I'm so proud of you." Flurry nudged her hand. "And you too, Flurry!"

Lori and another camp staffer made a seat for Arne by grasping each other's wrists to form a square. Arne put his arms around their shoulders. "Does this count as one of my Five New Things?" asked Arne ruefully.

"Generally they're supposed to be fun things," I said.

Arne nodded and then stopped, sucking in his breath in pain. Cassidy and I walked with Gwynn to the van, holding her hands.

"I got a sister brain message that you saw something scary," said Gwynn. "Like this." Gwynn let go of our hands and raised her arms, fingers curled and apart, and bared her teeth. "Raaaaar!" Flurry looked at Gwynn, mildly alarmed.

Wide-eyed, Cassidy and I traded looks. I hadn't told Gwynn about the mountain lion yet.

"Did you get any other sister brain messages?" I asked.

Gwynn nodded. "When you felt really, really sad, I sent a message telling you not to give up!"

I took Gwynn's hand again. I thought about the tiny columbine poking out between the rocks when we weren't sure how to start climbing over the rockslide, and how it gave me the courage to keep going. "I'm so glad we have sister brain," I said.

"I kept telling Arne and Mom that I would've gotten a sister brain message if something bad happened," said Gwynn. "But they were still worried. I had to work really hard to keep them thinking of other stuff. We named eighty-seven things that are purple! Do you want to hear? Eggplants, violets, amethysts—"

"We saw a mountain lion," I told Gwynn, interrupting her list. "I was afraid that it was going to attack Flurry. Flurry was ready to fight it!"

"And this happened while we were climbing over a huuuuge rockslide," said Cassidy. "And the rocks started falling again while we were up there."

Gwynn's eyes grew big.

"But we made it. And then I thought Flurry was going to get bitten by a snake," I said. "But it turned out to be Cassidy's scrunchie."

"Wow," said Gwynn. She squeezed my hand. "I'm so glad you didn't stop. Even when it was scary. I was getting thirsty."

"We just kept going," I told her. "Sometimes fast, sometimes slow. Sometimes crawling. But we didn't stop."

🌲🌲🌲

Arne had a broken tibia, which is the scientific word for shinbone, which led to a whole new thing for Gwynn. Now she wanted to be a doctor *and* president, so she started learning the names of bones. She found a book at home with a diagram of the human body and recited the names of the leg bones out loud: tibia, fibula, patella, femur. Mom says there are 206 bones in an adult human body, so that should keep Gwynn busy for a while.

After we got home, I called Kim and told her what happened—not just Flurry getting the last two skills, but our rescue mission back to camp. We were on a video call, so I could see her expression change when I told her about the mountain lion and Flurry finding the scrunchie. She was impressed.

"You've definitely fulfilled your end of the bargain," she said. "Let's figure out when you can come practice with us."

"I can't wait!" I said.

"Just remember, it's not going to be quite as exciting as what you've already done," said Kim, smiling. "But I think I have a few things to show you, and, of course, consistency is the key." That reminded me to work with Flurry on jumping on my back. I wanted to make sure she would do it all the time, not just when we were climbing over a rockslide.

Mom called Flurry, Cassidy, and me her heroes. When anyone asked how Arne broke his leg, she'd tell the whole story about how we made our way back to camp, adding in the parts that we told her about—the mountain lion, the rockslide, the scrunchie. If I happened to be there when Mom told it, she'd put her arm around me at the end and squeeze and say something like, "My amazing daughter, she can do anything." And then I'd stand there awkwardly while the other person made impressed sounds. Mrs. Faber, a regular customer at Kuai Le, said, "Oh Corinne! You should be proud of yourself!"

Was I a hero, though? I had done something scary, really *really* scary. But other things still felt scary to me, and I had not done anything about them.

One evening, I waited until Mom was alone. Gwynn was watching a movie, and Arne was in his office working. Mom was sitting in her bed with her laptop. I curled up next to her, being careful not to bump her growing belly.

"What's going on, Corinne?" asked Mom. "How's my hero-girl?"

It would have been so easy to just close my eyes and snuggle with Mom. But this growing feeling was becoming uncomfortable, like campfire smoke stinging my eyes. I took a deep breath. "I have something to tell you," I said.

Mom closed her laptop and set it on the nightstand. "Okay. I'm listening."

Just say it. Get it over with. Maybe Mom would be disappointed in me, but it couldn't be any worse than feeling like a phony.

"Sometimes . . . sometimes when we talk about the baby, I feel . . . worried," I said. "Will Arne love the baby more because it's his?"

"Oh!" said Mom. She gave me a squeeze. "Here's the thing—when you love someone, you just love them. There's no more or less. It just is. And the other funny thing about love is that it's not a fixed amount. There's always more to give. Did you love me less when we got Flurry?"

"No!" The thought of that made me laugh. "Of course not!" And then, just like that, the problem that I had built up in my head became smaller.

"It's the same with Arne," said Mom simply. "I might love different things about you and Gwynn and the baby, but I love you all the same amount."

I snuggled up closer to Mom. "I am excited about the baby," I said.

"Of course you are," said Mom.

"I just wish I knew how things are going to be different," I said. "Like a map of what to expect."

"I do, too!" said Mom. "But that's life, not knowing what to expect all the time. Like our camping trip! We thought it would turn out one way—"

"And it turned into something else," I finished. Suddenly I felt a push against my side. "The baby kicked me!"

"Ha! I felt that," said Mom. I wiggled around and put my hand on Mom's stomach. Another kick! "You were a kicker, too. I thought for sure you were going to come out a full-blown soccer player." Mom gave me another squeeze.

Who Rescued Who?

"I'm glad you decided to be brave and tell me how you were feeling. Sometimes that takes as much courage as hiking through the woods for help, or climbing over a huge rockslide."

I hugged Mom back. "Maybe more."

Three Months Later

Chapter 15

*P*lay with me!" whined Gwynn. "You can prep later."

"Just a second. I don't want to pack at the last minute. I might forget something." I was prepping a bag for another practice session with Kim in a few hours. Flurry and I had already gone on one, and Kim said after I went on a few more, we could start thinking about going on an actual rescue mission. I had a flashlight with extra batteries, a compass, and a bottle of water, plus a notebook and pen for writing notes. And of course, the C+C Survival Kit!

"Can you help me? I need to pack a protein bar," I said. Sending Gwynn to the kitchen would buy me more time to prepare. Plus, I really did need a protein bar!

Arne rushed in just as Gwynn stood up to go to the kitchen. "Girls! Get your shoes on. Molly just called from the restaurant. The baby is on its way! Molly's driving your mom to the hospital right now."

"Is Mom going to be okay?" asked Gwynn in a wobbly voice.

Three Months Later

"She is, but things are moving quickly," said Arne. "She didn't even want to wait until I could come get her."

I looked down at the bag I had been packing. "I'll call Kim and tell her we won't be able to make it today," I said. I felt a little giddy. The baby was coming! "I think she'll understand the reason."

"Yes, you do that," said Arne. His face was flushed and he kept looking around the room. "Oh gosh. A bag! Your mother hasn't even packed a bag yet. I'm supposed to get things. Like, um . . ." Arne looked at us. "A comb?"

"This is why I pack things ahead of time," I said to Gwynn. "See?" I patted Arne on the arm. "We'll help you. We can do it together."

🌲🌲

"Girls, wait for me!" called Arne. Gwynn and I slowed down to a run-walk. "Stop at the elevator!" We were in an extra hurry because it had taken so long to get to the hospital. Arne couldn't find his car keys because he had put them in the refrigerator! He was so nervous.

"It's not every day we get to meet our baby brother," said Gwynn. "Of course we're going to hurry."

Arne told us the room number and let us go in first. Mom was sitting up in the bed, holding a bundle in a dark blue blanket.

Corinne to the Rescue

A nurse smiled at us. "Congratulations!" she said.

Gwynn edged up to the bed and took a peek first. "Ooooh," said Gwynn. "He's squishy-looking."

"He came a little early," said Mom. "But he's going to be just fine and will unsquish soon."

Arne leaned over Gwynn and gave Mom a kiss. "You didn't wait for me!" he teased.

"Tell that to this little guy," said Mom. "He wasn't waiting for anyone!" She handed the baby to Arne.

Arne looked down at the baby and a huge smile spread across his face. "Oh my," he said. "Oh my, what a fellow." His eyes crinkled up.

I had seen that expression before—after I'd been rescued on the mountain. Mom was right. Arne loved me and Gwynn and the baby. More of us did not mean less love. It meant *more*.

Mom held out her free arm, and I stepped closer to let her encircle me. Arne leaned down so I could see the baby. Suddenly my heart felt as if it had filled up with a thousand beautiful and amazing things. Butterflies and rainbows and columbines. A night full of stars. Clean mountain air scented with pine.

"Wash your hands and you can take turns holding him," said Mom.

"What's his name?" I asked as Gwynn and I headed to the sink.

Three Months Later

"Blix," said Arne. "It means joy and happiness." Arne rocked back and forth on his feet.

"Blix Yong," Mom corrected. "Yong means brave."

"Brave and happy," I said. "I like it."

Gwynn held Blix first. Arne had Gwynn sit in a chair with a pillow in her lap, and then he handed her the baby. "Be careful now," he said nervously.

"I know." Gwynn traced her finger along Blix's cheek. "He's so tiny," she said. "Tiny and soft. Look at his little fingers!"

"You were like that," I said. "And then you grew!"

"Look," said Gwynn to Blix, pointing to her neck. We both wore the necklaces Arne had given us the day he married Mom. "See this necklace? It represents all the people we love. And now that includes you." She paused. "He's not opening his eyes."

"Babies sleep a lot," said Mom. "But I'm sure he heard you."

"He doesn't do much," said Gwynn.

"If you put your pinkie finger in his hand, he'll grab it," I said, remembering when Gwynn had done that to me. Gwynn slid her finger into Blix's tiny pink palm, and his fingers curled around it. Gwynn looked up at me and smiled.

"How about giving Corinne a turn with Blix," said Mom. Arne gently picked up Blix and set him in my arms. "Hi

little guy," I said. His eyes were still closed.

"Isn't it amazing to think that this is Blix's first day ever?" said Mom. "His first day meeting his big sisters and holding Gwynn's pinkie."

"Every day is Five New Things for Blix!" I said. "He still needs to meet Flurry, too." I started thinking of all the firsts that Blix was going to have—the first time seeing trees, or looking at stars, or paddling in a canoe. I was going to show him all the things I loved. Maybe I'd be the one to teach him how to ski switch or how to build a campfire. I could be Blix's mentor. I lowered my mouth to Blix's ear and whispered, just so he could hear. "I can't wait to show you the whole world."

Blix opened his eyes. "He's awake!" Blix's eyes were grayish green. They reminded me of the swirling waters of the river. He stared at me, and his small pink mouth formed an O. I think he was telling me he was ready.

I know I was.

Zoe and Margaret climb Mount Si.

Adventure
Buddies

Ten-year-old Zoe loves spending time outdoors with her adventure buddy, Margaret. They met in preschool and have been hiking, biking, camping, swimming, and skiing together ever since. "She's my adventure friend!" Zoe says. "We set lots of goals together."

One adventure goal they accomplished recently was to hike to the top of Mount Si in their home state of Washington. "It's only eight miles," Zoe says, "but there's a lot of elevation." In fact, the trail has an elevation gain of 3,150 feet. That's as tall as three Eiffel Towers!

To cheer each other on during hikes, Zoe and Margaret love to talk and sing songs. Zoe is a big fan of musicals like *Les Misérables* and *Into the Woods*, but the girls also make up their own songs. "When we were three, we made up a song that went like this:

Margaret and Zoe celebrate biking across Lake Washington.

'Three-two-one! Three-two-one! Time to get out of the house and sing three-two-one!'" Zoe says. The girls still sing it today! They also love to talk about their pets. Margaret has cats, and Zoe has a dog named Bella and a rabbit named Fluffo.

Besides their hike up Mount Si, Zoe and Margaret achieved another adventure goal last year. "We biked from my house to her house, which is seventeen miles," Zoe says. Their cities are separated by Lake Washington, and they had to bike over a huge bridge to cross it. And even though biking into Margaret's city was pretty steep, they had a lot of fun.

Their next adventure goal is to create their own

Feeling fine, rain or shine!

Ready to ride!

triathlon, which is a race that usually involves swimming, biking, and running. "We think ours will be nine miles of biking, three miles of walking, and then some kind of rafting," Zoe explains. But their triathlon won't be a race—the girls will work together and finish it side by side.

Nothing—not even cold and rain—can stop these friends from having fun on an adventure. It rains a lot in Washington State, so the girls are used to soggy conditions. That's why Zoe's advice to other adventurous girls is to be prepared with the right equipment. According to Zoe, "There's no such thing as bad weather, just bad gear! You have to be prepared for anything."

All Aboard the
Banana Boat

Make your own banana boats at home!

You will need:
-  An adult to help you
- Bananas
- Aluminum foil
- Toppings like chocolate chips, marshmallows, graham crackers, pretzels, and peanuts

Instructions:
1. Preheat the oven to 400 degrees.
2. With the peel still on, cut the banana down the middle.
3. Put toppings in the center of the banana.
4. Wrap the banana in aluminum foil and place on a baking sheet.
5. With an adult's help, bake for 8 minutes, or until the banana and toppings are soft.

133

Corinne Tan
1219 Farnam St.
Aspen, CO 81611
970-555-5555

A card with your
name and address,
and an emergency
phone number

Create
Your Own
Survival Kit

**Supplies to pre-
pare the bottle:**
- An empty vitamin
  bottle with the label
  removed
- 7–8 feet of 550
  paracord (available
  at craft stores)
- Masking tape
- Scissors
- Small carabiner

1. Tape the paracord
to the bottle,
with about 4
inches hanging
over the lid.

2. Starting at the
bottom of the
bottle, wrap the
paracord tightly
around the bottle.

Supplies to put inside:

Safety pins

Packets of antibiotic ointment

Matches and a strike pad, cut off from a matchbox

Adhesive bandages

Hair ties

1–2 feet of heavy-duty aluminum foil, folded into a small rectangle

Lip balm

Paper clips

Cotton ball (Add this last!)

3. Double-knot the strings together. Trim them if they're uneven.

4. Tie the strings again to create a loop.

5. Clip on the carabiner. Fill with supplies, and you're ready for an adventure!

MEET AUTHOR
Wendy Wan-Long Shang

Wendy's favorite things are freshly sharpened pencils, dogs, quiet mornings, good books, and the Spelling Bee puzzle in the *New York Times*. She wishes she were good at knitting and tennis, but has not quite devoted enough time to either endeavor . . . yet. Wendy writes about different aspects of the Chinese American experience through her middle-grade and picture books. She also wrote the novel adaptation of the Netflix original *Over the Moon*. She lives with her family in Falls Church, Virginia.

MEET ILLUSTRATOR
Peijin Yang

Peijin is a freelance illustrator who was born and raised in Tianjin, China, and now lives in Munich, Germany. She discovered her love for painting after college and started her art journey in 2017. Since then she has been creating illustrations for book publishers and working for various clients all over the world. Her personal artworks are also very popular and widely shared on social media.